# Charms and Changelings
## Astoria Wright

## Faerie Apothecary Mysteries
### Book 4

Charms and Changelings

Copyright © 2018 by Astoria Wright

Published by Novelwright Press, LLC
http://www.novelwright.com

Cover Art by Viyiwi
www.fiverr.com/viyiwi

Editing by 529 Books
https://www.529books.com

# Table of Contents

# Chapter 1

## Candy Hearts

Timothy Harbridge Jr. stared out the window of the Seelie Tree Apothecary shop. The chitter-chatter of his mother and Maren, the shop assistant, slid into the background of Carissa Shae's thoughts as she joined the eight-year-old boy sulking at the storefront. The half-elf apothecary tousled Tim's short, brown hair while pushing back a strand of her own frizzy auburn locks.

"Something wrong?" she asked, folding her arms to block the chill as the door opened for another customer.

Indoors, Carissa's pink sweater and red slacks were warm, but this close to the frosty windows, Timmy's long, blue winter coat made her wish she was still wearing her mint one hanging on the coat rack in the back room. The ringing of the bell above the entrance of the natural pharmacy finally ended. She gave a quick glance and a wave to the man, a local regular who was likely to peruse the shelves while complaining of a myriad of illnesses. Maren could handle that.

Carissa looked back at Timmy, thinking she'd gotten the better deal. However, she caught the storm brewing in the boy's eyes. He dropped his gaze a second later. Carissa generally found Timothy to be quick-witted and bright, but today his face had lost its color.

"I don't want to go to school. I dread it," Timmy said.

Carissa's elf ears twitched at the word dread.

"We all feel that way sometimes."

With a shake of his head, he rejected the sentiment.

"It's not just how I feel," he argued.

The boy's fists clenched and one sneakered foot pounded on the floor with an unintended squeak.

Carissa leaned against the window to get a better picture of his face. His features were as knotted as her stomach used to be on finals in her college days.

"Test today?" she ventured a guess.

"No." Timmy closed his eyes and sighed.

His adult-like exasperation was too amusing for Carissa not to crack a smile. Wasn't it teenagers who thought adults were too thick to understand them? Timmy was a bit young for that. And Carissa liked to think she was a bit more observant than other adults.

"Is someone at school bothering you?"

"No." He broke his gaze and studied the floor. "They're not bothering me, they're just...they're not the same."

Carissa crouched beside him so her brown eyes could meet his.

"Who's not the same?"

"Some of the kids at school. It's like...." He shrugged. Then, looking more adult-like than Carissa thought possible for a child his age, he fixed two serious eyes on her and lowered his voice, "It's like they've changed somehow."

Now she really did feel like a thick-headed grown up. She didn't understand what Timmy was trying to say.

"What do you mean?" she asked.

Timmy must not have found what he was looking for in her face. "You won't understand."

"Try me," she said.

He squinted at her. She thought it funny for a moment how seriously the small boy was sizing her up. The moment passed quickly. She cocked her head, noting the genuine distress on his face.

"Two of the boys at school, they're my best friends. I used to play with them all the time, but now they're not interested. They're playing weird games like sorting rocks and putting them in piles. They're not normal."

Carissa smiled. "Rock collections. I knew plenty of kids who had them. Maybe you could—"

"No," he said flatly. His fists were clenched again. "Not rock collections. Just rocks, like the ones on the ground. And they're always laughing at things that aren't even funny, like," his eyes searched the white checkered tiles on the floor, "like, I don't know, silly things—things people don't laugh at."

He said people like they weren't human or faerie, and there was an equal number of both on the island. Humans in any other place on earth might think the people of Moss Hill, or "Mossies," as the townsfolk called themselves, were strange just because they were accustomed to faerie culture. But, just like every society, big or small, it was always a difficult thing to find one's place in school. Carissa, as a half-elf, understood this well enough. She flailed for wisdom, explaining.

"People change as they grow up. That's just natural. I wouldn't worry about it."

Her reasoning had no effect on the child. Carissa looked away, uncertain what more she could say to reassure him. Her eyes skirted a stand full of trinkets beside the window. Maren's idea—souvenirs for tourists. There were plastic necklaces that came in two varieties: shining Valentine's hearts, and stars covered in what looked like faerie dust. All of them read: *My Heart is in Moss Hill.* Then there were candy heart necklaces. A couple of neighborhood children had bought those, but all in all, none of the jewelry, candy or otherwise, had sold as well as Maren or Carissa had hoped. Due to a glitch, they'd over-ordered the batch as well. At this point, they'd be selling them for years. So, giving one away wouldn't hurt.

"It's almost Valentine's Day," Carissa said. "Why don't you pick a pendant for a friend and one for yourself?"

Timmy shook his head. "It won't help anything."

A knock on the window jolted both of them out of the conversation. Outside, the puffy clouds had darkened, and hail was beginning to pound against the glass.

"It's getting dark," Carissa remarked, mostly to herself.

"It's like before." Timmy turned to her. "Remember? It got bad like this before, the weather. And the faeries were acting strange, but this time is different. Now it's the people."

Such fear and wisdom mixed together on Timmy's young face that Carissa couldn't ignore his warning any longer. Carissa bit her lip, staring at the mementos. She picked one up. Turning the star pendant in her hands, it played the light like a prism. Carissa held the jewel up to the window with one hand. Elf-light sparkled from the fingertips of her opposite hand. The necklace shone brighter.

"Here," Carissa said.

"What's that?" Magic lit Timmy's eyes.

"Elf-light for protection." She handed the pendant to her young neighbor. Whatever he was afraid of, the charmed necklace could offer protection. Carissa didn't think he really needed it. It was probably just school troubles blown out of proportion, but it wouldn't hurt for him to have it.

"When the world seems dark, a little bit of light can go a long way." Carissa winked.

"Timmy," Mrs. Harbridge's sing-song voice called to her son from across the store.

"Thank you."

Timmy took the necklace as seriously as a jeweler locking away a precious gem. He spun around to heed his mother's call, but before he could dash away, he paused. Turning back, he looked at Carissa with a question on the tip of his tongue. Carissa braced herself for whatever was troubling him next. Meekly, he scratched his cheek before asking, "Could I have a candy one, too?"

Carissa grinned. Worries or no worries, children were still children.

"Sure," Carissa said, and she stepped back so that Timmy could grab a candy necklace from the bin.

He took one with a spirited, "Thanks!"

Carissa barely kept from laughing.

The weather might've turned for the worse, but at least Timmy was feeling better. He slipped the necklace on before bolting to the center aisle, where his mother had made her way to the door.

"Thank you for the sleeping draught, Cari," Mrs. Harbridge said, opening the front door to let a chilly breeze inside. "The Cartwright's new baby is so loud we can hear him right through our bedroom window. Tim's been trying to get a good night's sleep for weeks...."

She continued to let in the cold while steaming about her husband, Timothy senior's, lack of sleep. Her son, however, seemed preoccupied with some sight outdoors. He clutched the pendant and his smile fell more the longer he stood there. Finally, the oblivious Mrs. Harbridge said goodbye, and the door closed behind her.

Carissa shuddered, her sudden reaction caused by the rush of air, the loud ring of the bell above the door as it closed, and the distressed look of the little boy that had gone entirely unnoticed by his mother.

"You'd better talk to someone about the heater," came a voice from behind.

Carissa turned toward her assistant, Maren Raines. Average in height and frame, but not in personality, the brown-haired assistant walked down the center aisle. "It's at least a few degrees different from one end of the store to the other, and you look as pale as a ghost. You're not becoming ill, are you?"

Carissa dropped her hand, which had reactively clung to her elbows. She ignored the goosebumps she felt beneath her sleeves and walked with Maren to the back counter.

"It's fine. The door was open too long, that's all," Carissa said.

Timed to the second, the door opened again. A ring of a bell and a breeze of winter followed Cameron Larke into the shop. Maren, perhaps wanting to give them privacy but also likely just noticing Mr. Burrows who'd come in a moment ago, uttered quickly that she would check to see if there were any customers in the Otherworld and disappeared. At least, she vanished to all but Carissa, who had already said the chant that allowed her to see into both human and fae worlds at once, as she was accustomed to doing every morning.

Maren was doing well with her newfound mastery of Otherworld travel. A month and a half of practicing with her Christmas present, an enchanted locket that allowed her to step into the faerie world at will, had given Maren the ability to part the veils and check on fae customers. Carissa already knew there were none but didn't begrudge Maren's desire to escape the unhappy Mr. Burrows. Besides that, she was happy with a moment to say hello to her boyfriend.

Cameron Larke, the tall, brown-haired, cognac-eyed liaison between Moss Hill and the neighboring faerie village of Vale, had won her heart over a prince—and it didn't hurt his pride to remember it more often than he should. Carissa rarely rolled her eyes, but whenever he came strutting into the shop with the charisma and charm of a politician, she couldn't help herself. It's not that he wasn't charismatic, quite the contrary.

She'd learned over time that he'd come into himself as his career had grown. He'd proven himself as a mediator who could handle the delicate negotiations between humans, sidhe, and elves—not to mention all the other faerie people who'd settled in with the Mossies. It was just that his work persona tended to engulf the rest of him.

"You're doing it again," Carissa said as he walked to the counter.

"What?" he asked.

"That thing with the face and the walking."

His head tilted in an eye roll of his own. "Fake Cam, the politician?"

"I never called you fake."

"No, but you 'prefer the real me,'" he quoted, "which is pretty much the same thing." He laughed.

"It's not the same thing at all." Maren, the eavesdropper, appeared from an aisle as if by magic.

Of course, it was magic, but the commonality of it in this town made it unimpressive to Mossies.

"Why not?"

"Because," Maren obliged, "it's you, but polished—usually for the press to get your best side." She reenacted taking a picture with her fingers. "It's not 'fake Cam,' it's 'camera Cam.'"

Cam cringed, and Carissa stiffened. The press was a bit of a sensitive subject since Carissa had thought for a while that Tilly, a blogger and town news columnist, had been interested in Cameron. The feeling, if it had been there, hadn't been mutual on Cam's part. He'd convinced Carissa of that, but Maren's innocent comment only reminded her that Cam's job involved a fair amount of contact with the beautiful and talented reporter.

"Well," Cam said, scratching his neck as he did whenever he was uncomfortable, "I'm hoping to put forth my best side right now because I would like to ask you, Cari, to be my date for a very special Valentine's dinner."

His growing smile gave away the fact that he was going to spring some surprise on her, but her eyebrows shot up and her face lit in delight when a bouquet of flowers appeared, floating in the air in front of him.

"What? How did you...?" Carissa was nearly speechless.

Humans could not perform magic. The exception was well-trained druids, but Cam was not one of those either. Three sprites popped out of the assortment of roses, asters, peonies, and daffodils with open arms as if to say "ta-da!" Maren gasped as the sight, but Carissa had never thought a sprite could disappear entirely—unless there was more to faerie dust than she knew.

Maren clapped and exclaimed, "Brilliant job!" while Carissa stared dumbfounded at the bouquet now in her hands.

Hiya, the boy nature faerie with his light blue outfit and broad wings, bowed. Chaos and Hiya's sister, Cynth, in their matching red dresses, shared an accomplished nod and drifted back. Each rested on one of Cam's shoulders.

Cameron beamed. "It's elfkin magic. Fudge showed me—well, I mean, he showed the sprites how to use it for simple things like this."

"It's beautiful," Carissa said, stretching up to kiss Cam on the cheek.

"So? What about dinner?"

Carissa laughed. "Yes, of course! Where are we going?"

Cam's smile widened. "Surprises," he said with a sparkle in his eye. "I'll pick you up at eight. I'd make it sooner, but I've got a feeling I might run late trying to convince the mayor not to make a rash announcement."

"What announcement?"

"None, if I can help it. He's just sore about the faeries in Vale taking jurisdiction over magical crimes in Moss Hill."

"Isn't he always?" Maren asked.

"Not so much that he threatens separation from Vale."

Cari's eyes widened. "He did what?"

"Nothing yet." Cam laughed. "He's just in a mood. I'll change his mind."

He walked backward, turning mid-step as he waved, and headed out of the apothecary shop to another busy day at City Hall. This left a clueless Hiya behind skipping across the boxes of supplements on the top shelves of the center aisle. Maren cleared her throat, and the boy sprite looked up, then frantically searched for his companions. Catching sight of the windows, he zoomed for the closing door and made it out just in time.

Chuckling ensued from one of the rows. Maren leaned backward, peering down the aisle to discover the source. With an incredulous brow and a dropped jaw, she came forward.

"It's Mr. Burrows."

Carissa released one hand from the flowers to cover her own open mouth. She was happy the old man was joyful, even as over-the-top as the laughter sounded. But what had sparked the change in him?

Old Mr. Burrows nearly skipped to the back counter. His eyes glistened, and he wiped his palm over them as the chortle softened to a sigh.

"They skipped over the sprite and left him behind, but he was a hop, skip, and a jump away from the door. Hee Hee!"

Maren and Carissa raised their eyebrows.

"Mr. Burrows, are you feeling all right?"

"Yes, yes!" he said. Then, he paused, seeing their expressions. He tugged at the hem of his coat. "I'm only laughing. Is that cause for concern now?"

"No," the two ladies said in unison.

Carissa tried to shake her head but ended up looking at Maren again. Quick on her feet, Maren walked their customer to the counter.

"Why don't I ring that up for you?" she said, pointing to the vitamins in his hand.

"Much obliged," he replied.

Shaking off the oddness of the outburst of joviality she'd witnessed, Carissa rummaged the back shelves for a vase. She reached for a pair of scissors and trimmed the stems of the flowers when a zap from her fingertips caused her to recoil. She rubbed her fingers with her thumb. It was more than static electricity.

Something had caused her elf-light to surge from her heart. She knew she had a strange feeling but hadn't realized how deeply she was feeling it. Despite the reaction in her hand, she couldn't pinpoint why she was feeling that way. She turned back, watching Mr. Burrows head out of the shop and thinking about Timmy's school problems.

So what if people were acting a little strange? It was normal for everyone to be a little abnormal sometimes. Experience had taught her that. Apparently, her emotional side wasn't logical enough to have learned.

She brushed it off, unwilling to play into the fears of an eight-year-old. It wasn't in her nature to ignore Timmy, but some concern existed only in the minds of children. At least, that's what she told herself.

# Chapter 2

## Parents' Heartache

The next customer to walk through the entrance, feet dragging, was a weary-looking Mrs. Anne Cartwright. The parent of the very same fussy infant Mrs. Harbridge had referred to earlier let go of the handle of the ocean blue door with sluggishness. But, the moment her eyes found Carissa, a surge of desperate energy seemed to envelop the woman.

Anne darted to the apothecary counter, taking down her hood to reveal her luxurious red locks. Her usually vibrant green eyes were set in dark circles, making her look far older than her twenty-something age. Carissa had seen sleep-deprived mothers before, but this was one step further. She wondered how she hadn't noticed given that Anne was not just a customer, but a neighbor as well.

"Good morning," Carissa's usual greeting was tinged with concern.

She couldn't utter a "how are you" before Anne started in on the reason for her visit.

"Carissa, I'm at my wit's end. I'm in need of a babysitter tonight. I feel absolutely terrible to leave her, but I thought if she's in your hands, at least I know she'll be well taken care of. Do you think you could watch Alayna tonight?"

The long-winded question threw Carissa. Of course, she'd watched over children before and even given health advice to parents as an apothecary, but her pharmacy training didn't include the actual care of a newborn. By Mrs. Harbridge's account, Alayna was a trying one at that. Though, anything that came from Patsy Harbridge tended to be greatly exaggerated.

"Sure, I'd be happy to," Cari said.

Anne closed her eyes and sighed like she'd just been resuscitated.

"Thank you," the woman uttered.

"Where is the baby now?" Carissa inquired.

Anne pushed a strand of hair from her thin face. "Her father took the day off, thank goodness. It's given me a chance to run some errands. I've got a million things to do before the day is out."

"Oh, Anne!" Maren, having gathered her items to leave for her shift at the bakery next door, exited from the hall where the back room was located. She brightened upon seeing Mrs. Cartwright.

"We've missed you at Sunday services," Maren remarked.

"We haven't been out much at all," Anne admitted.

"I understand. It must be hard with a new baby. How is Alayna?"

Again, Anne scratched her head and pushed back her hair. She seemed to fidget at every mention of her daughter.

"She's fine," she said unconvincingly. She must've realized her voice had betrayed her because she sighed and corrected herself. "Er, actually…she's not fine. She's been fussing—screaming, is more like it—and maybe…I don't know, she doesn't seem right."

Carissa straightened, asking, "When did her fussiness start?"

"A few days ago. But she's already two months old, and Alayna was so quiet before."

The longing in Anne's voice when she mentioned the word *quiet* was unmistakable.

"Have you taken her to a doctor?" Maren asked.

Anne nodded. "I've got an appointment for her with Dr. Larke this afternoon."

Naturally, Carissa's ears perked up. "She's an excellent physician."

The statement earned her a knowing look from Maren. Her friend might assume she'd only said that because she was dating Dr. Dana Larke's son, but Carissa genuinely thought well of her as she dealt with most of her patients.

Anne didn't look reassured, so Carissa leaned forward and rested a hand on her arm.

"I'm sure Dr. Larke will figure out why she's crying. When she does, bring her back, and we'll do what we can for her."

Maren, trying to be helpful, added, "Cari's right. It could be a cold or an ear infection or any number of things. Worst is colic, but we could treat that, too."

Carissa shot her a look. There was no need to put ideas in a new parent's head. Maren didn't seem to notice how Anne paled and repeated the word "*colic*" as if she'd just gotten a new idea to worry about.

Carissa tried changing the subject. "What time would you like me to come by?"

"What?" Anne asked.

"For babysitting," Carissa clarified.

"Around six." Anne put her hands on the counter. "Do you really think it could be colic?"

The question was…hopeful, which seemed odd.

"We won't know until Dr. Larke diagnoses her."

Anne seemed to take in a new breath. Then, surprisingly, she smiled. "I really let my imagination get away with me. Colic—that might explain it."

"Explain what?" Maren asked.

Anne shook her head. "I was beginning to think she was a whole different baby." She laughed, seemingly at herself.

"Exhaustion plays mind games like no other," Carissa said, lifting her hand now that Anne was feeling better. With a reassuring nod, Cari added, "I'll see you at six."

The tired mother seemed a bit more energized as she said goodbye. She skirted past a browsing customer and headed out the door.

Maren slipped on the wine-red coat in her hands and adjusted her brown hair as she remarked, "Poor Anne."

"Poor Anne," Carissa agreed. Then, noticing the clock above the door at five past 1:00 p.m., she asked, "Aren't you going to be late for your shift at Gooseberry?"

Maren tilted her head in the direction of the bakery next door and replied, "They'll wait. I want to stay until my replacement arrives."

Carissa held up a finger. "She's not a replacement, just extra help until the winter season is over."

"You might find her more skilled than me, considering her other employer."

Maren looked at her bag, adjusting it on her arm, trying for calm and collected, but Carissa could plainly see Maren's annoyance.

Holly's other employer was Macara, a powerful woman who served as the protector of Moss Hill. A member of the most ancient and powerful faerie race, the Tuatha de Danann, Macara had left the island to attend to urgent matters on the island of the King of Sidhe and Elves. Though Holly was a bean tighe, which was basically a nurturing leprechaun, she had gained knowledge in Macara's employ that might help Cari not just run the apothecary, but cope with the recent discovery that she, too, had a fae heritage that was part Tuatha de Danann. Since she barely understood her father's elfish powers that had passed on to her, she had no hope of mastering her other fae magic without help. Yet, Holly was not the assistant Carissa preferred at the Seelie Tree.

"She's not taking your job if that's what's worrying you." Carissa crossed her arms.

"I'm not worried," Maren put her hands up. "You had to hire someone, I understand. I'm only saying it was very smart to hire her."

"She was your idea."

Maren's palms opened wide, and she feigned innocence with her expanding eyes. "It's smart, no matter who thought of it."

Maren's self-appreciative tone was interrupted, but the chime of the bell in the Otherworld, which only Carissa could hear since Maren's skills hadn't yet progressed to the ability to see into both worlds at once.

In came the petite figure of Holly, the self-described bean tighe. The shop brimmed with the afterglow of the three-foot, middle-aged fae's pleasant smile. Her rosy cheeks matched her long paisley dress. Her red curls bounced as she bounded inside.

Carissa, realizing Maren couldn't see her, gestured for her to turn her locket and did the same so that both of them were now in the Otherworld.

"Good afternoon, lasses!" Holly's bubbly voice resounded through the store.

Maren and Carissa responded in kind, with Maren adding, "How are you today, Holly?"

"Very well!" The bean tighe brought a bag out from where it had been tucked under her arm. It had blended in so well with the dress it appeared to be made of the same material. "I've brought a few things, my dears."

She pulled out bundles of herbs and reached up to set them on the counter.

Carissa glanced between Maren and Holly, who was too busy with the bag to see her upraised eyebrow. "Um, thanks, but I don't think we need—"

"Oh, no trouble at all, dear." Holly set the last of the items on the counter and gave it two pats with her hand while looking up at Carissa. "You'll probably want to get those in the fridge. It'll keep longer in the cold."

Maren quickly turned her half chortle into a cough and cleared her throat. "So good of you to take my place while I work at the bakery."

"I'm glad to be here! With Macara away, there's no one for me to take care of—except Barnaby, of course. He overworks himself, the poor dear." She shook her head as she referred to the leprechaun tailor whose shop sat across the street. "Anyway, it's good for me to be out of the house."

Maren had to have noticed Carissa's tightly focused stare on her, which intensified with Holly's every word.

Outwardly, the assistant seemed oblivious. "Well, I know Cari and the store are both in good hands, so I'll be on my way. You two have fun."

Maren's smile was a dangerous mix of jealousy and gratification. Then, she turned her locket and disappeared into the Otherworld. To Carissa, Maren only appeared to change in hue as Cari could see the human world and faerie realm both at once as long as the magic of her double sight was in effect.

Carissa knew from the minute she said she needed to hire another assistant that she'd upset Maren. But, with Maren taking on more hours at the bakery next door, her assistant and friend should have understood that Carissa needed help during the ongoing flu and cold season. Maren's half-hearted offer to quit the bakery only made Carissa feel guilty. Why Maren had suddenly changed her attitude and suggested Holly for the job had been lost on Carissa until this moment. It became even more apparent as the bean tighe made herself at home once Maren left.

The sharp sound of metal scraping across the floor interrupted Carissa's slow realization. Holly dragged the stool they kept in the back corner up to the counter, raising herself to a good height over the flat surface.

"Now, I've heard quite a bit in town lately about sick children, and it's no wonder given the weather." The bean tighe stuffed her bag under the counter and rolled up her sleeves. "If you'll hand me the ginger, we can start on an excellent cold remedy that's been in my family for 1,200 years." She picked some rose hips out of the pile on the counter and sorted through the rest, looking for other ingredients.

Carissa obliged by walking over to the refrigerator, wondering the whole way whose store this was now. She had a feeling she'd just handed it over to an overly-enthusiastic faerie. She was so preoccupied with this fear that she literally bumped into a customer she hadn't noticed was there.

"Oh, I'm sorry," she said to the figure, who'd dropped a bunch of turmeric bulbs on the ground. "Here, let me help you."

The customer bent down and fumbled to pick up the items, muttering, "No, I've got it."

Grabbing one of the bulbs in each hand, Carissa lifted herself back up and handed them to the woman in front of her.

"Mrs. O'Brien?"

The words escaped her lips in a gasp, and she took a step without really realizing why. Mary was a usual customer, after all. She did look ill though, with the same sunken eyes and thin appearance as Mr. Burrows. Even her copper hair had dulled to a mousy brown.

She froze and looked at Carissa, then grabbed the tubers from her hand and uttered, "Excuse me," before rushing away from the aisle.

After Mary O'Brien disappeared around the corner, Carissa realized the problem. The woman's hue had changed to the misty colors of the Otherworld...but Mary was human. Carissa turned the corner to see Mrs. O'Brien again, this time more vibrant colors of the human realm.

Carissa blinked. Maybe her eyes had played a trick on her and she'd only imagined Mrs. O'Brien had been in the Otherworld. But, if that were true, she shouldn't physically be able to bump into her while she was in the Otherworld herself.

To test that theory, Carissa twirled the locket around her neck to slip back into the world that the humans occupied. She followed Mrs. O'Brien up to the counter and put a hand on her shoulder.

Mary turned. Her eyes darted between Carissa and the counter, and she dropped the turmeric onto the surface.

"I'll just take these," she mumbled, more gruffly than her usual soft-spoken manner.

Holly, if she was looking at both the human world and the faerie one, gave no indication that she could see her. This caused Carissa's eyebrows to shoot up even higher on her forehead. Trying for a professional appearance, Carissa caught herself and took a breath.

"Sure." She exhaled as she made her way around the counter.

"Don't take long, dear, there's an order to the recipe for the healing magic to work," Holly called, as if she were still waiting on the ginger.

That at least verified that Holly wasn't using her double sight to see both worlds at once. Carissa looked up at Mrs. O'Brien. She hadn't seemed to hear the bean tighe calling out. Mary even flashed her a smile, albeit a nervous one, before reaching for the bills in her wallet.

"If you don't mind me saying," Carissa ventured as she bagged the items, "you don't look well. Are you all right?"

The forty-something customer cleared her throat. "Just a cold." She grabbed her purchase, nodded her head, and smiled. "Good day."

"Have a good day," Carissa repeated absently while focusing on every line of her face.

She watched her go, but now Mrs. O'Brien seemed—other than a little sickly—perfectly herself.

Carissa thought about it a minute. There had to be a logical explanation, the most straightforward being that maybe her magic had glitched somehow. As a half-elf, she wasn't well-versed in magic—even her own.

Curiosity pulled her to the front door. Her eyes were fixed on the windows to see if she could get a glimpse of the receding customer when her feet crunched on something. She stopped and looked down. The entire entryway was covered in dust— a tan, sandy dust that should not have been there given the snowy conditions.

Carissa scratched her head. Could it have been a mix of mud and snow that had melted and dried? Was it faerie dust left here by Chaos, Hiya, or Cynth? She pondered the possibilities as she grabbed the broom.

By the time Carissa was finished cleaning the mess, she had concluded that Timmy was right. Something strange was affecting the residents of Moss Hill. She'd have to do something about it, just not tonight. Tonight, she had the pleasure of watching over a colicky infant. She almost preferred a mystery—even a dangerous one.

# Chapter 3

## Babysitting Blues

Something was wrong with the Cartwright baby—not wrong like a cold or the flu or even colic, but deeply, disturbingly wrong.

Carissa had arrived at 6:00 p.m. to Mr. Cartwright yawning at the door. The inside of the home was a bit unkempt, but Carissa could understand how the new parents might be too overwhelmed to clean. Even the porch had acquired some dust at the entryway. Mr. Cartwright himself was a bit of a mess, also. His blond hair was disheveled despite the fine brown suit he was wearing.

He greeted her with a lazy "come in," and proceeded to call to his wife. "She's here, Anne. Let's go, or we'll be late."

Carissa cocked her head. Anne hadn't mentioned what event they'd be attending. Based on James Cartwright's suit and the tie, Cari guessed.

"You have reservations for dinner tonight?"

James shook his hand in a jittery way, a rather unusual way to say no. "It's a formal gathering with the boss's family."

"The Greers?" Carissa asked, still standing in the entry hall but not taking any liberties in removing her coat or purse or entering farther inside. She couldn't anyway since he was blocking the way.

Finally realizing his manners, he gestured to the coat rack and stepped closer to the opposite wall. Then, he nodded, answering Carissa's question.

"Hotel's been doing well, despite, um...well, you know."

Carissa bit her lip. She'd been involved in Parker Greer's arrest, and while the mayor was a forgiving man, the sidhe had tried him for his use of magic. He was working off his crime in service in the fae village.

Mr. Cartwright cleared his throat. "Anyway, they canceled their Christmas party, and this is sort of making up for it, except it's also a briefing for a client coming anytime."

"Who is it?" Carissa asked.

James shrugged. "Some rich customer with special requirements. The boss wanted to speak with me directly about it, so I have to go."

Anne entered the room. Her distressed look from earlier was tempered with a forced smile. The fancy red dress, long earrings, and French twist hairstyle helped as well.

"You look lovely," Carissa remarked.

Anne gave a hurried "thanks," adding, "I've laid everything out on the dresser. There's some formula in the fridge if she needs it and here's the monitor." She handed a small white speaker to Carissa. "She's sleeping for now, but I don't know how long that'll last."

The nervous mother looked back toward the stairs.

"Don't worry about anything," Carissa said. "I've got it all handled. Did the doctor say what was wrong?"

The corner of Anne's mouth dipped. "Colic, maybe. He wants to see her again tomorrow."

"He?" Carissa asked.

"Oh, Dr. Larke had a mix-up with the appointment times. It was another doctor, Torro, Torgo, something like that."

"Dr. Torreng?"

"Yes, that's right. You know him?"

"I know of him. We haven't met. He's supposed to be very good. He treats Mayor Belkin and most of City Hall. Cameron speaks highly of him."

Cam couldn't go to his own mother since they were family, and his old doctor had retired. From what she knew of Dr. Torreng, he was not fond of herbal medicines and recommended patients to use the clinic pharmacy rather than Cari's apothecary shop. Cam was one of the few patients who did not take that recommendation. Still, he seemed to like the doctor well enough.

"I heard he was the mayor's physician. Mrs. Harbridge said he and Belkin were good friends. Well, I'm glad he saw us right away. I know it's not an emergency to have a colicky baby, but it feels like it sometimes."

Carissa tried a soothing tone. "If it is colic, there are some things we can do to help."

Anne and her husband replied with a "thank you," and both tried, unconvincingly, to look reassured.

The moment they left, the familiar generic ringtone Maren always chided Carissa for using rang out from her purse. She rushed to her chartreuse handbag, another atrocity according to her assistant, diving straight for the device. Carissa glanced upstairs and set down the baby monitor as she answered. No sounds came from the baby's room—not yet, anyway.

"Hello?" Carissa answered in a half-whisper.

"Cari?" a confused voice asked on the other end.

"Yes?"

The woman started shouting at someone else on her end. "What kind of contraption is this? I can barely hear on this tech-a-phone."

Carissa couldn't make out all of the reply, except the correction to "telephone" followed by the woman saying, "Well, you use it, then."

A male voice took over. "Hello, Carissa, sorry about this interruption to your evening."

"Barnaby?" Carissa said. "What's going on?"

"Nothing, Holly's just—"

"It's not nothing." Holly's voice was loud enough she didn't need to speak into the receiver.

Carissa's eyes flicked up to the ceiling again. Holly must've been next door visiting Barnaby. The leprechaun tailor lived with Timmy's family. In the human world, he lived in a room off the side of their kitchen, much like Nan's in the home Carissa shared with her. In the Otherworld, Barnaby had basically done up the whole house as his own. That might've concerned most humans, who liked their privacy, but Barnaby was one of the few fae who respected boundaries of the humans around him. It was probably why they were calling instead of just coming over.

"What is it?" Carissa asked as patiently as possible. She grabbed the baby monitor and walked back into the living room, still being mindful of the baby but now speaking at a more normal volume.

Holly continued her revelation. "Tommy's saying—"

"She means Timmy," Barnaby clarified. He must've been holding the phone between them because Holly's voice came in loud enough that Carissa pulled hers away from her ear.

"Anyway, he's saying children are acting strangely at his school. And the Harbingers—"

"Harbridges," Barnaby corrected again.

"Have just come from their store meeting."

"Moss Hill Business Association meeting." Barnaby sounded weary.

"Yes, well, long story short, there are more children coming down with illnesses. I think we'll need to be prepared tomorrow for an epidemic," Holly said.

"Epidemic?" Carissa couldn't keep the incredulity out of her voice. She was inclined to believe something might be going on, but from the brief time she'd known Holly, she'd learned the bean tighe could overreact. She could also be a bit overbearing.

"I've got a theory on what it could be, but we'll have to gather some special herbs just to test it. Now, I know I haven't been in Moss Hill for a century or so, but last time I was here there was a field just past Vale where…."

"Holly," Carissa tried to get a word in edgewise, "I appreciate your concern, but you're not even scheduled to come in tomorrow. If there's an illness going around, I'm sure Maren and I will have everything under—"

A sharp cry interrupted her. Carissa closed her eyes and let out a frustrated sigh.

"The baby's up," she said. "Hold on."

Carissa hastened up the stairs. She half-wondered if Alayna had heard Holly's panic over the phone. She hadn't been on speaker, but even so, the fae woman seemed to think she needed to shout to be heard. Carissa didn't blame Holly, fae generally didn't have experience with technology.

Holly's surprised exclamation didn't help. "Whose baby?"

Carissa winced, both from Holly's high-pitched squeal and the baby's shrill crying. Mrs. Harbridge wasn't lying when she'd said the child's crying was loud enough to be heard next door. She had to flick the baby monitor off for the sake of her ears. Carissa swore she could even hear the baby's voice from over the phone. She didn't worry about her own volume as she answered Holly's question.

"I'm at the Cartwright's, babysitting."

"Oh my, has it gotten to her too?" Holly asked.

"Has what gotten to her?" Carissa whispered hoarsely as she opened the nursery door.

"I don't dare say until I have more information."

Holly was finally speaking in a normal tone. Either that or the baby's cries were drowning her out.

"Hang on, I'll put it on speaker." Carissa couldn't believe she'd said that.

Still, she was almost grateful to have Holly on the line. A bean tighe might know what to do if she couldn't pacify the infant. She turned on the speaker and set the phone down on the dresser. Then, crossing the room to the crib, she cooed to the baby.

"It's okay, I'm here."

Carissa inched closer. She peered over the crib to see a mess of tangled blankets. Somehow, the baby had managed to roll around so that the sheets were overhead. Carissa gasped.

As if she'd heard her caretaker's frightened response, Alayna quieted. But this only scared Carissa more. Had she stopped crying because she couldn't breathe?

Purely on instinct, Carissa snatched the cover, hastily unwinding the swaddled cloth. It came away easily, but the sight beneath it gave Cari such a start that she stepped back and caught her breath. Fear and faerie light surged from her beating chest.

"Oh my—" Carissa started to say.

"What is it?"

"What's wrong?" Barnaby and Holly's voices came over the phone.

Carissa dropped the blanket in her hand and gathered the courage to approach the infant again.

"Is the baby all right?" Barnaby asked.

Carissa looked at the blueish-pale skin and piercing eyes staring up at her. The twisted smile sent chills down Cari's spine.

"She's alive," Carissa said, "but she's definitely not all right."

"We'll be right over," Holly replied.

The phone clicked off, leaving Cari to tend to the baby. This was not the little girl she'd seen at the christening two weeks ago. Baby Alayna seemed to find Carissa's bewildered face amusing. Her little laugh brought Timmy's words back to her in full force: "*They've changed somehow.*"

# Chapter 4

## Darlings and Danger

"Well, it's obvious," Barnaby said, setting his hat on the dresser while Holly scooped the baby into her arms. "She got herself all tangled up. She could barely breathe. Thank goodness you came in when you did."

He held Alayna's tiny fingers in his hand and rubbed his nose against hers. A giggle escaped the baby's now pink lips. A warm hue had returned to her cheeks, but the concern hadn't left Carissa's face.

"Her smile, Barnaby, you didn't see it. It was…different."

"She'd just been through a scare. She was happy to see you." He shrugged.

Carissa looked at Holly. The bean tighe was uncharacteristically quiet. Holly laid the baby on the changing table beside the crib.

Carissa asked her blankly, "What do you think?"

She studied the fae woman's face as she took out the baby powder while the baby played with the necklace hanging at Holly's neck. Alayna seemed to be concentrating intently on the heart-shaped gift Holly had received from Barnaby.

"I think the baby may need changing," Holly responded.

Carissa bit her lip. Of all people, she expected Holly to have given more of a reaction. Confused, Carissa wondered if she may have been letting her imagination get the better of

her. After all, Holly knew more about magic and children than
Carissa did and she didn't seem concerned.

Once the baby was changed and placed back in the crib,
safely swaddled by the skills of a bean tighe, the three of them
retreated. Carissa checked that the baby monitor was on again
before closing the door behind her.

Holly must have seen Carissa's preoccupation because she
placed a hand on her arm and nodded, then she led Carissa
and Barnaby downstairs. In the kitchen, Holly put up a kettle.
Carissa set the baby monitor at the center of the table while
Barnaby tried to reassure her.

"Holly knows what she's doing. She's taken care of an
infant or two in her time."

Carissa frowned as she dragged a chair from the table. It
was true that she had all the book learning but lacked
experience with infants. Still, she knew something was wrong
with Alayna, and it wasn't colic.

Carissa also knew that swaddling ought to end by the time
a child was old enough to roll around in the sheets, but Holly
had not only swaddled her, she'd also tightened the cloth as if
it were a restraint. And it hadn't escaped Carissa's attention
that Holly had waved a hand over the girl to put her to sleep
magically.

Alayna's parents didn't have the luxury of magic to care
for their child. They were doing their best, but if something
magical were going on, they would need help from faeries like
Holly. Carissa tried again to convince the bean tighe.

"Holly, you were saying that there is an epidemic in Moss
Hill."

"That's right, dear," Holly said.

"So, what if this is a spell? What if something is changing
people's behavior, even their health. You know about the
unseelie." Barnaby flinched at the word, but Carissa kept on.
"What if a dark fae is responsible for this?"

"Oh, I think a dark fae is definitely responsible for this."

"You do?" Barnaby and Carissa asked in unison.

Holly nodded. She picked up the whistling kettle and took a painstakingly long time to pour the liquid into three cups. She remained as cool as a cucumber while handing them the hot tea.

"Well?" Barnaby inquired.

"Who's responsible?" Carissa held her hands out as much to take in Holly's knowledge as to take hold of the cup and saucer.

"I can't," Holly shook her head, "not until I know for sure. She swore she'd change her ways. I'm the one who persuaded the Sidhe Council to let her live in Vale. How will it look accusing her of going right back to the unseelie ways? No, no, I can't possibly."

Holly patted Carissa's hand. "We need to gather the herbs. They grow in her field, but she'll give them to me right away, I'm certain of it. She'll want this cleared up as much as any of us."

"Who?" Carissa asked.

"Oh no," Barnaby said, shaking his head. "You're not talking about Teg?"

"Who?" Carissa asked again.

Holly shot Barnaby a stern look. "She goes by Tabitha now, and I hope you won't repeat that."

Carissa ignored the fact that Barnaby would most certainly repeat everything he heard now and asked anyway. Her curiosity was piqued.

"Who is Tabitha and what would she have to do with this illness?"

Holly shook her head. "It's probably not her, but if it is, then it's not an illness."

Her eyes drifted into thought as she sipped her tea. Barnaby took her distraction as a chance to lean forward and whisper to Carissa.

"Tabitha is the daughter of a bendith y mamau, a dark tylwyth teg," he said.

"What's that?" Carissa whispered.

"I can hear you," Holly said, and clanged her cup down with annoyance. "Don't go filling her head with nonsense."

"It's not nonsense, it's the truth."

"Busy tongues make broken truths." Holly wagged her finger wagged at the leprechaun.

He dug in his heels, or rather, dug a spoon into the sugar bowl at the center of the table. "It's not a broken truth. And I'm not saying it's Teg's, er, Tabitha's fault, but it's all right for Cari to know. Macara did leave her in charge of Moss Hill's protection, after all."

Holly's eyes lifted from Barnaby and settled on Carissa. A few seconds passed before the bean tighe sighed and took up her cup again.

"All right, I suppose you have a point." She took a sip and daintily lifted a napkin to her mouth.

For someone so loving, she had a way with suspense that bordered on torture.

"A tylwyth teg is a beautiful faerie, even more so than elves. But, their beauty comes from goodness. If they can't find goodness in themselves, they find it in others and use it to bring out the beauty in themselves. They can do this through kindness or coercion. That's when they become a bendith y mamau. It translates roughly to 'mother's blessing.'"

Carissa shook her head. "I don't understand."

Holly reached toward Carissa's idle teacup. The liquid was getting cold, but she didn't much care. The bean tighe heated it with her hand, a light orange glow emanating from her palm. Then, the fae pointed.

"The way the warmth in a cup of tea can warm your heart—that's how love works. A tylwyth teg loves her family and friends and is beautiful for it. A tylwyth teg turns evil when they feel they have no love, so they kidnap people, mainly children full of beauty, and keep them as their own. The children come to love her. Love warms her heart so that she can love them in return. Since love changes you from the inside and makes you more like the other person, it changes her to be beautiful, too."

Carissa enveloped the tea with her hands. She hadn't realized how frozen her fingers had become. She breathed in the scent of rosehips and exhaled.

"I'm sorry, I still don't get it. Couldn't she just be loving toward others without kidnapping? A person doesn't need to steal a child to have love in their lives."

Barnaby fidgeted, and he looked at Holly like he was preparing for a storm.

"The twylyth teg are related to goblins, who have never been accepted into sidhe society. There's a long history there I'd rather not get into, but the point is it gives some of them a complex, so they always worry about being left out." Holly glanced at Barnaby, who looked as if he thought she was brewing a tempest in a teapot. Holly retorted before he could even start. "Tabitha is a bit odd, but she doesn't deserve to be so ostracized."

"The tylwyth teg have their own community," Barnaby said to Carissa. "They don't really like other fae, and they have plenty of kindness between themselves, which keeps them beautiful as ever." He turned to Holly. "And it's not that we don't like Tabitha, Holly. What are we supposed to do? She lives in a hut outside of Vale, and she likes it that way. She doesn't associate with us, not for our lack of trying. Hela tried visiting her last week, and she threw toadstools at her!"

"Now, I don't believe that," Holly said, "unless she insulted Tabitha somehow."

Carissa didn't know what to make of that. She knew Hela to be good-natured on the whole, but she was also a bit of a spoiled elf who didn't always think before she spoke. It wasn't inconceivable that she could insult another faerie accidentally. That wasn't what was important at the moment, though.

"Can you prove that it's not Tabitha?" Carissa asked.

Holly nodded. "The toadstools are both a food source and a source of magic the bendith y mamau use to whisk away the children. I can make a potion from the toadstool to test what type of changeling magic is being used—if any." She pointed at Barnaby. "But I don't want you to say anything until I can use it to find out once and for all if that's what's happening here."

Barnaby nodded. "If there's a dark fae to suspect, I think Tabitha's a strong possibility, but I won't say anything. I didn't see anything wrong with Alayna anyway." He sipped his tea and silenced himself on the matter.

Carissa was sure the silence would break the minute he met the first person he could tell about Holly's suspicions. But, maybe he'd resist his temptation to gossip for once. After all, it was Holly who was asking.

"We'll collect the toadstools tomorrow morning before the shop opens," Holly said to Carissa. She rose, picking up her and Barnaby's cups.

"I'll come, too." The leprechaun wiped his mouth before standing.

"No need, we'll be fine," Holly said as she took the cup and saucer over to the sink. She paused. Her hands came away from the dishes now floating in midair. Her finger rested on her bottom lip. "But there is someone else we might want to bring along."

"Who?" Barnaby asked.

"A troll changeling," she said, "and I just happen to know one who lives in town."

# Chapter 5

## Toadstools Are Red

Mr. Crimbal was a meek man. If he was fae, it was hard to recognize him as such. He spoke with such careful acumen and in such a soft tone that Carissa didn't notice he was there until his shadow loomed over her head.

"Excuse me, may I inquire why you've asked me to meet you on the road to Vale this morning?" he asked with his hat in his gloved hands.

It was cold enough to see one's breath this morning, but he was dressed for it, with what looked like multiple layers over a checkered brown coat and caramel scarf. He was tall and slim, which made the jacket droop over his shoulders. His thin, grey hair seemed to be going everywhere. Carissa tried to keep from staring.

"Mr. Crimbal," Holly chirped, "I'd like to introduce you to Carissa Shae. She tells me you've never met, but I think you may have heard of her apothecary shop?"

He bowed. Carissa stuck out her hand at the same time, then dropped it awkwardly and nodded instead. Thankfully, he replaced the hat on his head, and she could focus on his face. His eyes were as dark as Sal's, but the bulbous nose was a contrast to the elfkin's sharp, pointed features.

"Yes, I think everyone in Moss Hill has heard of the shop."

"Have you been in before?" Carissa asked.

"No," he said, looking to the mountain. "Are you planning on going into Vale?"

"Yes, and I'd like you to come with us."

His already pale skin lost even more of its color.

"What business would I have there?"

Holly smiled wide, ignoring the question by turning to the trail. Her abundance of personality was an effective tactic for evasion.

"It's a chilly day, isn't it?" She started walking. "And a long way in such weather, I wonder if you could lend me an arm."

Mr. Crimbal obliged, but he wasn't put off by her attempt to change the subject. "I don't see why you called me to escort you."

"Don't put yourself down, Otto. You're fine company. Tell Carissa about your job. It's fascinating, Cari, really."

Crimbal glanced sideways at each of them and frowned. Carissa's eyebrow dipped in sympathy. She had to admit that she was intrigued to hear what a troll might be doing in Moss Hill, especially since she'd never heard of a troll who wasn't an unseelie.

"I'm a financial advisor," Mr. Crimbal replied.

Carissa smiled.

"She knows what I am?" Otto asked Holly. He didn't wait for an answer before asking Carissa, "Think it's funny for a troll to work in finance?"

Carissa's lips settled back down and she shook her head. She was the one who paled now, embarrassed at her stereotypical thinking. It *was* funny, though. Trolls were supposed to be the greediest people in the world, fae or human. They hoarded whatever others found valuable for the simple reason that others found it valuable. In this world, that meant money, of course, because nothing was more valuable to humans than that.

"Oh, don't be offended, she didn't mean anything by it," Holly said.

But Mr. Crimbal straightened. "I make my money honestly. I made the wealthiest families in Moss Hill, and they trust me implicitly."

Carissa felt her muscles tense as Otto's tone changed. The pale skin had made him seem meek, but Carissa could now see that mild wasn't the right description for him. Temperamental might be more like it.

He trudged along with Holly, feet dragging, though that might've been due to the layers of snow crushing beneath their weight. Carissa felt a knot forming in her stomach. Her attempt to fight her nervousness resulted in a wavering smile as Crimbal glanced back at her and then increased his speed. He seemed nervous too.

Walking with a nervous troll and a bean tighe to the home of a former unseelie fae in the middle of the Vale woods wasn't a typical start to a day, even in Moss Hill. Carissa tried to make it one by way of light conversation.

"So, Mr. Crimbal, have you been in Moss Hill all your life?" Carissa tried not to outright ask about him being a changeling, though Holly hadn't explained and she was curious.

"You mean when was I switched with a human child?" Crimbal's eyes flicked between Holly and Carissa.

"No use bringing up old grievances," Holly's cheerfulness felt out of place.

Her use of the word "grievance" was especially odd. Whose grievances did she mean? Crimbal's for being a changeling? Or the family he'd been placed in for having their child switched with a troll?

"I'd rather it be answered and done with entirely." Otto turned to Carissa. Holly's arm was still locked with his, but Cari increased her speed to walk alongside him. "The humans found me out and regained their child, but only after five years had passed. By then, I had formed an attachment with the humans around me—not the boy's family, but a doctor, who took pity on me and saw great potential in me. He took me in when the trolls were banished from the island."

"When the trolls were banished? That was two hundred years ago."

"Your point?" Crimbal asked, his eyebrow raised.

Carissa bit her lip. She had to remember she was dealing with a faerie. She didn't know how long a troll's lifespan was, but she probably shouldn't have shown surprise that his age would be different than a human's.

"Um, never mind," she said. But then a question appeared clear as the road in front of her. "How do you know the tylwyth teg?"

Mr. Crimbal's eyes darkened, and his skin seemed to take on a blueish hue, much like Alayna's had the night before. It was odd how this changeling appeared to fit the term itself so perfectly. He was unstable in nature, changing in appearance and tone with the topic.

"The Mossies thought she ought to be the one to raise a changeling, but she refused."

"Then why—"

"Why would Holly want me to come with you to see her? She didn't tell me her plans beforehand or I might not have agreed to come, but now that I know the destination it's obvious. My magic is similar to the tylwyth teg's: changeling magic. Should she prove to have gone back to her old ways, I would be able to protect you. I can see that you're surprised. Yes, I know troll magic. I was determined to learn to control my own powers, even if no faerie would agree to teach me."

"Past is past," Holly said, "and it ought to stay where it was put—behind us."

There was more behind them than the past at that point. The whole road to Moss Hill had gone by with little notice on Carissa's part. Yet, they were already at the entryway to the Village of Vale.

Where the road ended at the base of a steep incline, Holly used her magic to shift them into the Otherworld. To human eyes, they would seem to disappear, from Carissa's vantage point, the world took on that subtle dreamlike hue. The hill before them became a set of stone steps, and she moved toward them, familiar with the entrance to the faerie village. Holly caught hold of her arm.

"Not that way," the bean tighe said.

Holly and Crimbal diverged left to a path that may or may not have existed under the snow. They seemed to know exactly where they were going. Carissa couldn't help but glance around for signs of faerie life.

She knew there were fae who lived outside of the village—faeries like Noz, the bugul-noz who was civil but socially awkward. Then there were the duergars, whose mischief-making was meant to mislead humans. This especially included tourists who were not supposed to know of Vale's existence. But all the fae around this mountain were seelie, and therefore would never do real harm to anyone—or so she'd always believed. To discover that an unseelie, even a former one, resided so close to the human town and faerie village was unnerving.

It was hard to know what to expect when they came upon a dwelling in a clearing on the other side of a hill. The thatched-roof cottage was surrounded by a picket fence with red toadstools popping up all over the snowy yard. Pink smoke rose from the chimney as if greeting them.

At the gate, Holly let go of Crimbal's arm and waved a hand above the latch. The gate swung open by her magic, and the three travelers stepped inside.

Immediately, a voice boomed out over the area. "Set one more foot on my ground and suffer my wrath!"

"If your wrath is that horrible toadstool soup you served me last time, I imagine I can suffer through it, but I'm not sure about my companions," Holly said.

The door of the cottage opened, and a hesitant speaker appeared. Carissa flinched, her hand flying to her lips. The tylwyth teg was…green. A green woman as tall as any human and with long, silky blonde hair stood in the doorway. Her face was sharply defined. Her floor-length, lavender dress was faded, but her vibrant eyes made up for that. They glowed as she tilted her head to study them.

Carissa couldn't tell if she was beautiful or ugly. Both at once, she supposed. One thing was sure: this fae was fearsome to behold.

The tylwyth teg held out her hand, a clear signal to stop moving. Carissa flinched. A cloud of grainy purple faerie dust rushed at them. Carissa's arms formed an "x" over her face, and she coughed at the sand-like magic. Holly patted her back, and Crimbal's brows chided her as he shook his head. He seemed to have expected her to be prepared for this, but how was she supposed to know if Tabitha would strike at them with her magic? Wasn't Crimbal supposed to protect them?

Tabitha took a step down from the doorway. Carissa inched backward. She wouldn't be caught unprepared again. The tylwyth teg was smiling. Her skin changed to a warmer tone, more golden than green. She reached out to embrace Holly in a hug.

"It is you!" Tabitha seemed genuinely delighted. She kept an arm around Holly's shoulder, but her face contorted upon seeing Crimbal. "And you," she said to him. To Carissa, she said, "And you are...?"

Unsure what to do, Carissa dipped, not low enough to be considered a curtsey and yet not definable as anything else.

"I'm Carissa Shae, ma'am."

The tylwyth teg curled her fingers around Carissa's cheek and turned her head left, then right. "I don't see it. Wait, no, there it is. Yes, I see it now. Gareth Shae's granddaughter right there." She pinched Carissa's cheek as if that were the exact spot in which she could be identified as a Shae.

Tabitha let go of her shoulders. "Toadstools." The way she said that reminded Carissa of the way one might say "good golly" or "goodness gracious." Tabitha continued, "My manners are a bit dusty." She chuckled at her own joke, referring to the faerie dust she'd blown onto them. "I've no visitors to use them on."

"That's not true," Holly said. "I heard the head elf's daughter visited you just last week and was welcomed by a bunch of hurled toadstools."

"Toadstools," Tabitha repeated. "Was that Hela? I thought it was a sneak. Or is Hela a sneak? Prying into my business."

"What business is that?" Crimbal asked.

Tabitha pursed her lips. "None of yours."

Carissa looked back and forth between the staring contest the two fae had begun. Holly tried to pacify the situation by clearing her throat.

"You've not offered to let us in," Holly reminded the tylwyth teg.

Tabitha unfroze and scanned their shivering bodies. She nodded, uttering a quick, "Come in," while turning to the door. "Now, what was that you said about my toadstool soup?"

***

TABITHA OFFERED AN abundance of unappetizing foods one after the other as if launching them at her guests.

"Fairy butter," Tabitha said, placing a tub of something yellow and gooey into Carissa's hands.

The fae sifted through more items in a large bin Carissa assumed was her form of a refrigerator.

"I don't have any flower petals to spread them on, sorry." Tabitha's slender fingers tapped the edge of the box as she peered inside.

Carissa gently set the tub of fairy butter on the table in the tylwyth teg's kitchen and looked at Holly. Crimbal walked right out of the room in a huff. Carissa leaned back to see where he was going. To the couch in the sitting room, apparently.

"Your home is not quite what it used to be," Holly said, brushing a finger on the wall and holding it up to show Carissa the dust.

Tabitha closed the food box and twirled back to the bin.

"Many things are not what they used to be," the tylwyth teg said. A faraway look came into Tabitha's eyes, and they flashed brightly before fading. They were the oddest shade. Carissa sometimes thought they were blue, sometimes purple, and other times black. "I'm not what I used to be," Tabitha remarked.

"Well, we can help you with that, dear," Holly said.

"No!" Tabitha's sharp reply caused Carissa to shrink back.

So far, Cari hadn't said or done anything, but this woman's behavior was odd, and they didn't seem to be learning anything from her.

"We were hoping you could help us," Carissa said. "Some of the Mossie children are...ill...and we think there's a plant in your garden that could help us."

"Ill children?" Tabitha clutched the fairy butter like it was a bundled infant, holding it tight. The fae woman looked at Holly. "That's why you've come?"

The hurt in her eyes was unmistakable. Holly took a chair and looked up at Carissa.

"Would you give us a moment, love?"

Carissa didn't like the idea of leaving Holly alone with the eccentric fae, but she nodded and slowly retreated to the room where Crimbal sat. She found him gazing down the hallway as if he'd seen a ghost. The floorboard creaked. Crimbal turned. He threw her a disinterested grimace as she crossed the room.

"Disgusting," he said.

It took Cari a minute to determine he was talking about the state of the house and not Carissa's arrival.

"I thought tylwyth tegs were supposed to be good caretakers," she replied.

"They are," he said, "but Tabitha's been on her own too long. She's gone a bit goblin, I think."

Carissa ignored the remark. It was an insulting stereotype to think all goblins were slobs, especially since she'd found out that her friend Sal was half-goblin. The servant to Head-Elf Rolin was anything but messy. Still, Carissa had stereotyped

Otto for being a troll working in finance, so she supposed it was hypocritical to be offended.

She joined him at the edge of the room and peered down the eerie, dark hallway.

There was no sound coming from the supposedly empty parts of the home. Still, if Tabitha had kidnapped any Mossie children, she might have used a concealment spell to muffle their cries. There could be hidden children in any one of the bedrooms. Carissa glanced back at the kitchen. The rise and fall of Holly's voice could be heard, which meant Tabitha was likely still preoccupied with the bean tighe. Carissa took a step forward.

"I wouldn't do that," Mr. Crimbal said.

"Just a quick look," Carissa replied.

"It'll be a quick spell, too, that knocks you out cold for who knows how many hundreds of years, and I can't promise I can save you from it." He leaned closer to her. "There's no magic like that of the changeling kind—that I can guarantee."

Carissa shrank under the eyes of the troll. She shuddered when Holly entered the room, breaking her gaze on Mr. Crimbal. He straightened, and Carissa tried to do the same, but she knew some of her fear lingered on her face.

"Well, dears, Tabitha has agreed to help, so we'll get the fungi and be on our way. Tabitha, love, it was a pleasure to see you. You are welcome to visit me anytime."

Tabitha stood in the doorway of the kitchen, holding her hands together in front of her and smiling at them. She nodded as each one passed her toward the door.

Carissa was the last of them to leave. When she came to Tabitha, she nodded and gave a nervous smile, then swallowed and looked down, hurrying by the tylwyth teg. But Tabitha caught her arm. Carissa felt a jolt of elf-light leap from her heart, but it was dissipated by the tylwyth teg's cloud of magic swirling around her fingers.

The fae leaned forward, whispering right into her ear, "Don't trust him, whatever you do." Then, she let go.

Carissa rubbed her wrist, looking Tabitha in the eyes. The swirling purplish shades were impossible to read. It left Carissa to wonder about her all the way back to Moss Hill.

She kept her eyes on Mr. Crimbal, who was silent and stoic the whole way back. Was he the one Tabitha meant? He was a changeling, but she was a bendith y mamau…how could Carissa know who to trust?

She knew one thing: there were people in Moss Hill she trusted implicitly. If she wanted to solve this mystery of all the changes in townspeople and children, she would have to rely on her friends. She bit her lip as a frightening thought entered her mind. What if her friends started changing, too?

# Chapter 6

## Love Letters and Alarm

"Reginald sent a letter!" Maren practically danced into the shop, hugging the envelope in her hands.

She stopped when she saw Holly propped up on the bench, concentrating on a concoction. Her mouth hung open, and she looked up at Carissa with a puzzled expression.

"Well? You were saying about a letter?" Holly said before Carissa could respond.

The bean tighe did not look up from her work. There was no look Carissa could give or subtle words she could say that would convince Maren to ignore the faerie woman's presence.

"Holly, I didn't know you were coming in today," Maren said.

"It was an emergency, dear."

Carissa shook her head. She did not have to look at Maren to know that her alarm would have increased with that statement.

"An apothecary emergency?" Maren spoke slowly, pausing between each word.

The first customer of the day walked in the door, triggering the bell. The customer had to squeeze past Maren to enter the store. Maren stepped farther inside, but now that there was another person in the shop, Holly couldn't explain what she was doing here today without the possibility of the customer overhearing.

Carissa finally interrupted. "I'll explain later. You were saying something about a letter from Reg?"

Maren's lips thinned for a second, but she recovered by the time she made it to the counter. She set the paper down along with her purse.

"He says Hy Brasil is beautiful and he says hello to you and Cam and everyone." Maren looked at Holly while saying "everyone." The hostility was lost on the busy bean tighe.

Maren put the rest of her items down, and the customer bought his bottle of ginger-spiced lozenges.

"Did he say anything about the Tuatha de Danann?" Carissa asked.

They had gone to the land of the origin of the faerie races specifically to speak with the most powerful and ancient of the faerie ancestors: the people known as the Tuatha de Danann. Their request was to protect Moss Hill against infiltration by evil faeries known as the unseelie. It all started with a rash of strange events and crimes, and a note from a mysterious woman called Ms. Raven Corvus, warning them that the unseelie were returning to their cozy island town. Now, the threat had escalated to a possible invasion.

"Not specifically." Maren shook her head and frowned. "He did say that I should be careful, though, because they caught an unseelie trying to sneak into Hy Brasil. They're questioning her, but one thing they know for sure is that she snuck on to the boat in Moss Hill, pretending to be a servant to the king. She was hiding in Moss Hill as a human under the name O'Mally. We don't know how long she's been here, but he's worried there might be more like her because she kept saying that when her family finds out they caught her, the people of Moss Hill would be sorry."

"Can I see the letter?" Carissa wouldn't have asked, but the revelation Maren had just made seemed too important to ignore.

"Do you think she has family here in Moss Hill?" Maren asked.

"We already know the unseelie are trying to get into Moss Hill. It's not surprising," Holly said.

"It doesn't say what type of fae she is," Carissa handed back the letter. She wondered if any of what was happening now was connected, and she voiced that concern to the others.

"We can find her by the name," Holly assured. "I'll see if Barnaby knows any fae by that name."

"I can ask Cameron to search the records at City Hall," Carissa said.

Maren tried to be helpful as well. "I'll write back to Reg for more information. Varick said one of the sidhe elders is traveling back to Hy Brasil tomorrow. Did I tell you Varick was the one who brought the letter to me?" Maren walked into the storeroom to set down her purse and coat and walked back as if there'd been no interruption in her conversation. "That felt strange, a sidhe guard captain delivering a letter. Actually, I think he might've been using the letter as an excuse to visit Moss Hill. I hear he and Jane are back together."

"They are," Holly nodded. "He wrote her the most romantic letter. I caught a glimpse of it on the coffee table when I was visiting last. It said mortal or immortal, Varick didn't care, as long as he could see her, he'd take every second with her he could get."

"Ooh, that's good." Maren rested two elbows on the counter beside the bean tighe and rested her head in her hands. "What else did it say?"

"Really?" Carissa asked. "Don't you think it's a little wrong to pry into their privacy like that?"

Maren and Holly both blinked absently at Carissa. With her hand on her hip, she knew she looked like a stick in the mud, but did everyone in Moss Hill have to share everything about everyone else?

The two resumed their chatting. Carissa just shook her head and walked away to see what needed restocking or reorganizing.

She needed to think anyway. On the way back from Vale, she'd decided that she would not only ask Cameron for help but Alden as well. As Grim Reaper of Moss Hill, he wasn't likely to be replaced by a changeling. It seemed impossible, in fact. She wasn't sure how the ankou could help, but maybe he could spy on Tabitha or Mr. Crimbal. But which one? Who was more likely to be the cause of the changeling epidemic? Holly's test would prove whether the children were human or fae, but she'd told her once when they were back in the shop that it would only detect changeling magic. Tylwyth teg and troll magic were apparently indistinguishable when it came to changelings. Holly didn't seem to think it was either of them. Maybe the best bet would be to find out more about the O'Mallys instead.

Carissa continued this train of thought for a minute or two before the bell above the door rang again and in walked not one, but three women. Carissa recognized them all as regular customers and was prepared to smile and greet them, but it seemed like they weren't here as shoppers but as mothers.

"Is it true?" the tall brunette in the red coat asked.

The shortest one in a red checkered jacket said, "We heard the children are being replaced by changelings!"

"What are we going to do?" the blonde woman in yellow cried.

Holly's jaw clenched tighter and tighter as the panicked women spoke.

"Excuse me," she said through her teeth while jumping off the stool. She strutted around the corner of the counter and straight to the door.

"Where are you going?" Maren asked.

Holly called back, "To see a big-mouthed leprechaun about a broken promise!"

Without the bean tighe in the shop, the women zeroed in on Carissa.

"Is it true that there's a bendith—uh...," the short woman started.

"A bendith y mamau," the blonde intervened. "We heard there's one outside the fae village who's taking the children."

The women continued for some time, debating whether they should go to the Moss Hill authorities or the sidhe guard. They seemed determined to set someone on Tabitha. They weren't even entertaining the possibility of her innocence.

Finally, Carissa opened her mouth. "Hold on, you're jumping to conclusions. All we know right now is that some of the children are getting sick, and we don't know why."

"They're more than sick. My Dara says that some of the schoolchildren are acting odd."

"So does my Wesley. What if this fae comes for my children next?"

Carissa's lip might have bled with how hard she bit into it. Maybe she would have to send Alden to Tabitha's home after all. If the tylwyth teg was guilty, he would need to investigate. If she was innocent, she might need protection.

# Chapter 7

## Charmed and Dangerous

As with any small town, Moss Hill gossip spread like wildfire and was difficult to extinguish with logic alone. Maren had only fanned the flames of rage, gasping upon hearing for the first time the possibility that there was a fae outside of Vale kidnapping human children. Carissa's reassurances that this was most likely not the case did nothing to calm the alarm of the young mothers. So, the quick-witted apothecary had to rely on the second best asset against their heated arguments: her charms.

In this case, the charms were literal, of the magical variety, in the form of the heart- and star-shaped pendants enchanted with protection spells. Since the tokens for tourists hadn't sold well, there were more than enough charms for the three mothers to give to their children. Carissa suspected they'd be handing them out to the whole town by the end of the day.

"We shouldn't be gifting them, we should be selling them, Cari. They weren't free, after all," Maren whispered while she worked on the enchantments for the three worried women.

"I'm not charging parents to protect their children. I don't even know if the protection spell will work on changeling magic," Carissa replied.

"Of course not, just the cost of the necklace. We have over a hundred!"

Carissa frowned. They had over a hundred because Maren had mistakenly ordered twelve dozen instead of twelve total. The vendor refused to take back the extra 132, and now they were stuck.

Of course, today, that might be a good thing.

"We'll have to take the loss. It's worth it if it helps."

Maren, however unhappily, had to agree when Holly returned to the shop.

"Insufferable leprechaun!"

"Barnaby admitted to telling about Tabitha?" Carissa asked.

"Just the opposite! Denied it to the very end. We had a right-big row."

"But if he didn't tell, then who did?" Maren asked.

"Oh, don't believe him. He's a troublemaker. If you knew him when we first met, well, you'd know."

Carissa knew what Holly meant. Barnaby had once told her that he had been considered a nuisance in Vale. He liked practical jokes, played tricks, that sort of thing: the trouble of youth. The sidhe had banished him from the village, but he was different now; Mrs. Morgan had straightened him out.

"He's changed," Carissa said. "He's not a troublemaker anymore."

Holly stopped dragging the chair back to the counter long enough to raise an eyebrow. "You mean he isn't the town's biggest gossip?"

Carissa shared a glance with Maren. She couldn't argue with that point. Once Holly finished moving the stool, she climbed back up to the counter.

"What's this?" Holly asked. The necklaces strewn across the counter crowded the workspace where she had been creating her potion.

"Charms," Maren answered.

Carissa explained, "I thought the children could wear them, something to protect them from…whatever might be affecting them."

"Hmm." Holly picked one up, inspecting it. "Charmed with what?"

"An elf-light protection spell." Carissa showed Holly by charming the one in her hands. "It's one of the only spells I know. My dad taught it to me when I was little. He said if everything else failed me, it was the only spell I'd need."

"Did he?" Holly smiled. "Wise elf." She set the necklace down.

"Will it work against changeling magic?" Carissa asked.

"I imagine it should." Holly set about combining the herbs she'd crushed earlier. Using a bit of magic, Holly swirled the glass bottle. The herbs blended into a liquified, charmed potion.

Maren set her elbows on the counter, arms folded.

"Amazing!" she exclaimed while leaning in close. She looked back up at Carissa. "Why do I never see you do magic like that with your potions?"

Carissa shrugged off the words with a smile. Maren wasn't always aware of how her words could sting. It wasn't her fault. Most of the island residents had fae blood going far back in their ancestry, but it was different being half-fae. What good was it to be a descendant of a Tuatha De Danann when Carissa had grown up as a half-elf who'd never learned proper magic?

"Is it changelings, though?" Maren's question pulled Cari out of her thoughts. "Carissa said you weren't sure."

"We'll know soon." Holly stuck a cork in the top of the bottle. The potion was ready. With one hand holding the bottle and one on the back of the stool, the bean tighe hopped down with surprising agility. She reached for her bag from under the counter.

"Where are you going?" Maren asked, standing up.

"We," Holly replied, "are going to see a sick baby."

The bean tighe took a few steps before stopping and turning around. Carissa had taken a few steps toward the back room to get her purse, but Holly's voice pulled her back.

"Well, come on, girl, get your things and let's go. Cari, mind the shop, won't you?"

Carissa stopped in her tracks. *Mind the shop?* She looked at Maren's blank expression.

"You want me to come with you?" Maren asked.

Holly clasped her hands together, her bag on her arm, looking the picture of a middle-aged fae. "If it is a changeling, I'll need a quick pair of hands to help me catch it."

Maren cocked her head, clearly not understanding what the fae woman was talking about. She looked at Carissa, who didn't know any more than her assistant.

Holly gave an exasperated sigh, much louder than it needed to be to make her point. "Some changelings use magic to escape—they run away once they're found out."

"But it's a baby, isn't it?" Carissa said.

"Not necessarily. With changelings, you never know. If it is one, it could be anything from an older fae to a lump of clay pretending to be a baby," Holly said. "Oh, stop standing around with your mouths open, both of you."

"But why me?" Maren asked.

"Carissa has her charms to make, unless you know how to enchant a protection spell onto the necklaces?" Holly replied.

"Is it even safe for me to go? I don't have magic."

"Here." Carissa held Maren's locket in both hands and infused it with her faerie light. "This should protect you."

Holly tapped her bag lightly. "You won't even have a use for that. I've got all the magic we need. You'll be safe, I promise."

Carissa said a nervous goodbye to the odd pair and watched them until they disappeared from the apothecary window. After a moment, she turned and walked straight into the back room, leaving the shop floor empty. She retrieved a small bag from under the desk where the computer sat and took a pinch of the herbal mix from inside. Flat in her palm, the herbs ignited in a flash of elf-light and disappeared as Carissa uttered the words, "Show thee, ankou."

She waited.

Not a second passed before a spectral form appeared behind her. It was always behind her, never in sight. As usual, she flinched at the first sign that Alden was there. Alden, the ankou, apologized—as he did every time.

"Sorry." Alden's face shifted back to human form the second he came face to face with her. His blue eyes gripped her even as he stepped back. They were clear and sad and hauntingly illuminated.

"It's all right," Carissa said. She'd stopped asking if he could, just once, make a less startling entrance.

She really shouldn't be surprised anymore, and she didn't have the time anyway.

"We've got a problem," she began, but barely had the words out of her mouth before the ring of the bell came from the front of the shop.

A few footsteps resonated.

"Hello?" a voice called out.

Carissa dipped her head in frustration. "Sorry, I'll be right back."

Coming around the corner, she was met with an unexpected sight. A man in a tan shirt and pants of the same material with a tool belt around his waist and a clipboard in his hand stood by the door, glancing around. He looked familiar, but Carissa couldn't quite think of his name. She approached him curiously.

"Can I help you?"

The man walked midway through the center aisle to meet Carissa.

"Actually, I've come to help you. I heard you had some type of problem," the man's statement caused Carissa's eyebrows to raise, but her expression changed with the addition of three more words, "with your heater?"

Her eyes closed in relief. Of course. Maren must've called for a repair service yesterday after her complaint about the temperature at the front of the store. Now that she understood why he was here, she could also place his name.

"Mr. Hart, yes, well, no. Maren exaggerates. I'm not sure it's broken, maybe it's not as effective as it used to be."

"Same problem at Gooseberry," he said. "I've just come from there. Seems someone left strict orders to come here afterward and give an estimate for a repair. Doesn't hurt to take a look. Should I?"

That sounded like Maren. She must've talked the owner there into a repair, and she'd keep complaining until Carissa did the same. She had no choice but to let the man take a look.

"System's in the back. Thanks," Carissa said.

She rethought that statement the moment she said it, realizing a certain Grim Reaper might be a shocking surprise if Mr. Hart passed him on the way. She turned to utter, "Wait!" but stopped at the sight of a man in a black hooded jacket and dark pants standing at the counter with his back to them. Mr. Hart didn't seem to pay him any more mind than he would other customers. He trudged to the end of the store, made a right, and disappeared down the hall.

Carissa walked to the back of the store. Alden lifted his head as she resumed her place behind the counter. He spoke quietly, removing his hood.

"I don't think you've called me here for a heater. What's the other problem?"

Carissa kept her voice at the same level. "What do you know about changelings?"

Alden looked up, thinking for a minute before shaking his head. "It matters what kind."

"I know there are troll changelings and the tylwyth teg—"

Alden waved a hand. "That's not what I mean. There are a few different races who use changelings, but there are three types of changelings they use. They may be their own children. Fae sometimes send them to be raised by humans. Fae children are often more difficult to handle than human children, so it's easier to raise a human child as a servant and leave poor unsuspecting humans to raise their unruly children. Then, when their own children are at an easier age to manage, they bring back their child and then they have their own child and a human servant."

"Or they abandon their own children, like Mr. Crimbal," Carissa said. She shook her head at Alden's confused expression. "Never mind, I'll explain later."

He paused but then continued. "Fae also use inanimate objects—mud, stones, things like that and magically shape them into human form. But they're not real, so they look ill, and, eventually, they die."

"The Cartwright baby was ill, but there was something else. There are people around town acting strangely. Timmy noticed it at school."

"There are also older fae, faeries in disguise. It's an infiltration technique. The unseelie use it to get into homes and places they couldn't get to otherwise."

Carissa's eyes doubled in size. That's what Holly had meant. The first two types of changelings weren't likely to run away. Holly might've thought she had enough magic to take on a fae, but without knowing what type of changeling it was, she was taking a risk and putting Maren's life in danger, too.

"You could have started with that—" Carissa grabbed her phone from her pocket. Urgency rose in her voice. "You need to get to Crescent Circle right away. The address is 274, across from my home to the right. Holly and Maren have gone to check in on a family whose baby might be a changeling. Go, watch over them, just in case."

Alden replaced the hood on his head.

"I'll keep them safe," he promised as he disappeared.

The moment he was gone, Carissa turned her attention to her phone. She didn't need to dial since the number was always on the list of her recent calls. Cameron answered on the first ring.

"Hi, Cari." His casual tone reassured her that at least all was well at City Hall.

"Cameron—"

"Uh oh, you're not canceling tonight, are you? Because I've got it all planned—"

"No," Carissa had to stop him before he rambled on and spoiled his own surprise. "What makes you think that?"

"I know you, Cari. You only use my full name when you're upset. What's wrong?"

She knew she shouldn't be smiling under such serious circumstances, but she liked that he knew her so well.

"Cam, I need you to search the town records to find a woman named O'Mally. I don't know the first name. She snuck onto the boat to Tir-Na-Nog so it would be someone who hasn't been seen since the king's party left."

"A human snuck onto the fae king's boat?"

"I think she's a fae who was pretending to be human," Carissa responded.

"I can check records, but if it was an unseelie in hiding, she might've covered her tracks. I've got a meeting with Rolin in an hour. I'll tell him about it...unless I shouldn't?"

Carissa's lips fell. She knew why he was asking. She had a distrust of the fae hierarchy in the past, but Nan said she was too untrusting. She took too much onto herself when she ought to trust others to help. She wanted to listen to her grandmother's words this time, but the feeling nagged at her again.

"Tell him, but if you're going to be in Vale, find Varick, too. Tell him he might want to place a guard on Tabitha's house—that's a fae who lives outside the village. Some of the humans are under the impression that she's responsible for putting some of the children in danger." She held back the rest. It was too much to tell over the phone and part of her was aware there was still a repairman in the shop.

"The children? Are they okay? What did she do?" Cam asked all three questions in rapid succession.

Carissa raised her hand as if he could see her. "We don't know, maybe nothing's wrong, and maybe she's not responsible. I don't want to accuse her if she's innocent. Varick is the only sidhe guard I trust to give her a fair investigation. I'm a little worried about what the townsfolk might do if they're scared enough. You should've seen their anger earlier, Cam. I don't think there's anything more dangerous than a desperate parent."

"I'll tell Varick. It was Tabitha, right? And what was the name of the other one?"

"O'Mally," Carissa said. She noted movement to her left and saw Mr. Hart approaching from the corner of her eye.

"Got it. I'll look into it. Are you all right, though?" Cam asked with a level of concern only a boyfriend would feel.

"I'm perfectly fine," she replied, her smile reflecting her gratitude for Cam.

She hung up and turned her attention to Mr. Hart. He placed his clipboard down on the counter.

"So, what's the verdict?" Carissa asked, slipping the phone back into her pocket.

"Everything's in working order, only needed some adjusting."

"And how much does that cost?"

Mr. Hart put up a hand. "No worries, love. It's not technically a repair, just maintenance."

"Are you sure I don't owe you?"

"Really, it's fine." He clasped the clipboard between his arm and chest and nodded a "good day" to her, but it occurred to Carissa that she could repay his kindness.

"Mr. Hart," she called, using her elf-light discreetly before he turned around. "You have a daughter, don't you? You could give this to her for a Valentine's Day present—no charge."

She handed the necklace to him. There was no need to tell him it was enchanted; the protection spell would work without him needing to panic about a changeling incursion.

He smiled. "Thanks."

He stood there, weighing the heart necklace in his hand like he had something weighing on his mind. Carissa tilted her head. Before she could ask, he scratched his head and began.

"Um, I wasn't going to ask about it—I don't like to pry, you know, but I heard you talking about Mrs. O'Mally a moment ago. Do you know if they found her yet?"

"You know her?" Carissa asked.

She didn't wonder at his second question. If she was going by Mrs. O'Mally, she must've been known to the residents here, and it would seem like she'd disappeared. If that were the case, then the Moss Hill authorities would have made a record of her disappearance. That meant Cam would at least find something on her.

He set the clipboard on the counter and leaned forward, speaking low even though there was no one in the shop. "She's an odd one." His face twanged with guilt. "I don't mean to be rude. I'm not one to gossip, but you've got a sweetheart at City Hall, and I just thought maybe I should say something…."

"What is it?" Carissa asked.

"I don't want to get involved, so if you won't say who said it…."

"I promise, Mr. Hart." Carissa set her hands on the counter. "Go ahead."

He took a second longer to make up his mind, but the shadow of doubt passed over him soon enough. "You know she was a cleaner at the school, right? The kids said she didn't talk much. My Jenny kept away from her, but right before she disappeared, Jenny said she saw her by the schoolyard turning from a human right into some type of creature."

"Or a fae?" Carissa asked.

"See, I said that. I told Jenny maybe she's a fae who made herself look human around the children, so as not to scare them. It wouldn't be impossible 'round here. But, Jenny said she was no fae type she'd ever seen before. I passed it off as nothing, but now I don't know. I keep wondering why she was hiding it. And then she went missing. Do you think it's connected?"

Carissa held her tongue. All she could offer was a broken smile and a shrug. Anything more and her elf-nature would make it difficult to lie. Mrs. O'Mally was most definitely fae, and an unseelie one at that. That was why she was hiding her real self—she didn't want to be recognized as fae. If she was human, then her disappearance might alert the Moss Hill authorities, but it would definitely escape the notice of the sidhe guard. Humans were not their jurisdiction. Mrs. O'Mally might've taken that into account, but she hadn't counted on getting caught or on Reg sending a warning letter.

"I didn't want to say anything," Mr. Hart repeated, filling in the silence. "It's not my business if she's fae or human, I know that, but it just seemed strange, that's all. I do hope she's all right."

"What is Mrs. O'Mally's first name?"

"It was…let's see…Tara…Tam…Tamsin? Yeah, I think that was it."

"Thanks," Carissa said. "I'll mention it to Cam."

"Do you think it's important? Do you think it'll help with the investigation?"

"Maybe. We'll see what happens."

# Chapter 8

## Heart and Home

A hundred pendants and a few additional customers later, Carissa closed up shop and headed home. She tried to call Maren again. Alden hadn't returned, and Cari hadn't heard from either of them since they'd left. She hated worrying. The work was time-consuming, but not distracting enough to keep her mind from conjuring worst-case scenarios.

It was a little early to leave, but she threw the pendants into a tote, grabbed her purse, and pulled the coat on one-handed.

"Come on. C'mon," she whispered into the phone as she hurried through the apothecary shop.

Once again it went to voicemail. Carissa ended the call and shoved the cell phone in her coat pocket. She'd already left three messages. It was no use.

Her hand found the key, and she locked the door without even thinking. Her mind traveled to Crescent Circle, and she discovered much worse in her imagination than she hoped would be there in real life. Using her elf-magic to speed up her journey, she rode home as quickly as she could.

Once she arrived at Center Circle, she stopped opposite her home at the house with the rose bushes outside marked 724. She jumped off her bicycle, feet practically flying to the door. She rang. It felt odd, ringing and waiting after her mad dash here. The elf-light pulsed in her hands. She closed them into tight fists, ready for anything.

James Cartwright opened the door as wide as the grin on his face. He still looked tired, but now there was something else in his eyes: happiness.

"Hello, Cari! Anne, it's Carissa," he called back into the house.

"Well, invite her in!" came the cheerful voice of a contented mother.

Carissa hesitated.

"So, everything's all right?" Carissa asked, not budging from the doorway.

"More than all right!" Mr. Cartwright walked backward, making room for her to enter. "It's you, Holly, and Maren we have to thank for it." He turned around and kept walking so that Carissa had no choice but to follow him inside. She did so, cautiously.

In the living room, she found a radiant Mrs. Cartwright, holding her infant daughter in her arms and walking back and forth. She showed Carissa Alayna's face. It was round and full with just a hint of pink warmth to it: a perfectly healthy child. Her eyes were closed, contented. Her little chest moved in a steady rise and fall.

"She's asleep." Her mother's eyes were shining. "I can't bear to put her down."

"Whatever medicine you made, Carissa, thank you," Mr. Cartwright said, wrapping an arm around his wife.

Carissa could hardly believe it. She took a moment to find her voice.

"It was Holly," she said, finally.

She wanted to be happy for them, but this picture of domestic tranquility was incomplete as long as her friends were missing.

"Do you know where Holly and Maren went? After here?"

"They said they were going to a fae doctor," Anne replied.

"They could've done that differently, though." James showed the first sign of annoyance in saying that. His tone of voice earned him a consoling look from his wife.

Anne explained, "Holly and Maren were in the room upstairs. They said they needed a minute alone with Alayna to examine her. I put on a cup of tea and James waited with me."

"More like paced back and forth." James seemed to be trying to make light of the situation, but it was clear it had bothered him.

Carissa forced a faint curve into her lips, but whatever was making James seem upset made her dread what they might say next.

Anne continued, "We heard a bit of noise, like a crash. So, we darted up the stairs to see what had happened."

"Holly had gone," James said.

"But Maren was still in the room. She said that the baby had turned suddenly ill and not to panic, but that Holly had rushed her to Vale for treatment. Then she left, too," Anne explained.

"All in a hurry like she was scared to death. I didn't appreciate that one bit. You don't rush off with someone's baby. That's kidnapping." Before James could rant further, Anne calmly resumed her summary of events.

"Maren said not to worry and that the fae have cures our doctors don't. She went after Holly. James and I were naturally upset, but we trust Maren, of course." She glanced nervously at her husband.

"I nearly called the authorities," he said bluntly. Then, he sighed, rubbing his forehead with a hand and closing his eyes. He opened them and looked at Carissa. "I know you're half-elf, but all this crime lately, the talk of unseelie, it's unsettling. I know it's Maren and I know Holly works for you, but you have to understand, it's our child."

Carissa put up a hand. "You don't have to explain. Any parent would feel that way. But how did Alayna come back?"

Anne kissed Alayna's forehead, and James picked up one tiny hand in his fingers. Then his eyebrows knotted and he looked up at Carissa. "You don't know? She only just reappeared a minute before you rang the doorbell."

"She was just upstairs alone," Anne said. "We heard a soft crying, and there she was, just as she'd been before she was ill. Absolutely perfect."

Anne was smiling, but James was not. His wife didn't seem to notice the strangeness of the situation to the same degree as he did. He scratched his head.

"We assumed it was faerie magic—like a transportation spell or something." He sat on the edge of his seat. "Are you saying it's not? Is there something else going on here?"

Carissa shook her head, trying not to alarm him. He hadn't used the word "changeling," so he must not have heard the news around town. But she wasn't going to bring it up, not when it seemed they had gotten their little girl back.

"No, I'm sure that was it. I'm glad Alayna's all right now," Carissa said.

James visibly relaxed.

Anne didn't seem to pay enough mind to their conversation to have sensed any prior tension.

"When you see them, tell them 'thank you' from us, will you?" she said.

Carissa nodded. The happy mother looked down at her child like she was never going to let her go. All appeared to be as it should. Carissa stood up.

"I should go," she said.

She turned. Mr. Cartwright stood, too. A troubled look in his eyes returned.

"I'll see you out," he offered.

At the door, he stopped Carissa, speaking in a hushed tone.

"There was something wrong, wasn't there? I mean, deeply wrong, like," he looked back at the living room, then again at Carissa, "it wasn't Alayna before, was it?"

Carissa paused, cocking her head to the side. Had he heard about the changelings after all? If he hadn't, he would eventually, wouldn't he? She still wasn't going to confirm or deny it. She didn't really know the truth, not for sure, anyway.

"Why do you say that?" she asked.

"Something Maren said, that we would finally have our daughter back, not that she'd get better, but that she'd be back. That means she was taken, not by Holly today but by…something else before like a changeling…wasn't she?"

Carissa glanced between him and the opening in the hallway. Whatever had happened before, she could see from the smile on Anne's face that everything was all right.

"It doesn't matter now, does it? She's safe, that's what matters."

Carissa gave a kindly nod and smile, then turned toward the door.

"Wait!" James whispered.

He gripped her arm and immediately released it. She turned back to see the look on his face. He was worried and maybe just a bit sorry for what must've been an instinctive reaction.

Carissa didn't ask what was wrong, just looked at him.

"I overheard something at work. Something between Mr. Greer and someone else…the guest at the hotel—the one with a whole slew of guests coming into her party. I don't know who she is. She wants her privacy, we're not allowed to know who it is, but she said, 'Our sister's family is larger still,' something like they'd never seen sunlight and that they were upgrading from 'a hovel to Moss Hill.'"

"So the client used to be poor? Her family is moving to Moss Hill?" Carissa shook her head, not seeing the relevance.

"But I heard a rumor from one of my waitstaff about changelings. Don't changeling creatures, trolls and things, don't they live in hovels? And the client has all sorts of odd requirements: darker curtains, root vegetables only for food, and no high heat. They want the heater turned lower than we were keeping it. Mind you, the Greers never kept it warm enough in winter—penny pinchers. Anyway, what if this client, whoever it is, what if they're planning on taking over?"

That confirmed that he had heard about changelings. Like everyone else in town, it must've crossed his mind that a changeling had targeted his child. Only in his case, it may have actually been true.

Mr. Cartwright's voice had risen as he'd spoken. The fear in his eyes had inflated them, and the bags under his eyes were more prominent. Carissa wasn't sure if he was on to something with the guests at the hotel, but she did know that James's weary mind would trouble not just him, but anyone with an ear to listen if she confirmed his hypothesis.

"They could be fae." She shrugged. "But then, I'm half fae, Barnaby's a leprechaun, and Gilly down the road is a brownie. It doesn't necessarily mean these visitors are unseelie. They didn't say they were taking over the town, just coming here." Carissa tried nonchalance, but she wasn't even convincing herself. She could see her words weren't doing much to soothe Mr. Cartwright's nerves, either. "Tell you what," she said, "I'll ask Cam to look into it, just in case. Why don't you get a proper night's sleep in the meantime? Rest always gives me perspective."

"Perspective, right." He rubbed his eyes wearily. "Oh, maybe I am blowing things out of proportion. Thanks, Cari, for everything." He said goodbye, looking somewhat more relaxed than before.

Carissa walked back to her bicycle, not feeling relaxed at all. She picked it up off the ground. Cari knew she hadn't locked it, but had she really just tossed it down? She puzzled over it for the ten seconds it took her to cross the street and secure it in her driveway with her elf-magic. Then she tried calling Maren.

No answer.

She texted a few lines to the effect of *call me ASAP.* Then she hurried inside, hoping they might be waiting there for her. She opened the front door and pushed her way inside, finding it difficult to get through. The air seemed stiff somehow, like walking through a wall of water. She came out on the other end disoriented.

"Mind the barrier, Cari, it's strong for sprite magic."

"Strong for what?"

Carissa kept a hand to her head and stumbled into the sitting room. She took a seat on the sofa chair closest to the door before she could make sense of her surroundings.

"I should've warned you, dear, but I wasn't expecting you home this early. Cup of tea and you'll come right out of it." Her grandmother held a cup and saucer in front of her.

The scent of chocolate tea slowly pulled her back to her senses. Carissa felt a tug on her shoulder. Two nature faeries pulled at her bag, trying to dive in and see. Nosy sprites. Carissa set the bag on the floor. It wouldn't do any harm for them to look at the necklaces, but she gave them a warning anyway.

"No magic on those pendants," she warned Hiya and Cynth.

The boy and girl faeries nodded before eagerly opening the tote. At least things inside the house seemed normal. Carissa reached out and took the cup and saucer from her nan.

"What was that?" Carissa asked.

Nan resumed a seat on the sofa, explaining, "Protection spell. Chaos cast it on every entrance. It protects against all magic but only lets the seelie inside. Timmy here has Chaos up in arms about an invasion."

Her grandmother spoke as if the whole thing were vaguely amusing. Timmy, on the other side of the room in his blue school uniform, sat cross-legged on the floor with her tablet on his lap. He looked worried, quite the opposite of Nan.

"When is my birthday?" he asked Carissa.

"What?" she replied.

The tea might be bringing her 'round, but the question had put her off again. Chaos patted Timmy on his cheek while Nan reassured him.

"If she was a changeling, she couldn't have made it past the barrier. I'm sure it's her."

"We can't be sure. Changeling magic is tricky. It says so here." He tapped the screen. "Sorry, Cari, but you have to answer. When is my birthday?" Timmy demanded again.

Carissa had to admire the determination. "April seventh. Now, if you don't mind, please answer my question. What on earth is going on? And how did you unlock my tablet?"

The boy gave a sheepish half-smile. "It wasn't my idea. Chaos knows your password."

The nature faerie knew she was in trouble. She had already flown behind Timmy's back, disappearing from Carissa's sight. Cari would reprimand the nature faerie later. Now, she was more concerned about Timmy.

"All right, but why all this talk about changelings? Where did you hear that word?"

"It was Chaos," he accused the faerie again. "I was coming home from school, and she could see I was upset. I told her what was wrong and she dragged me in here. She had the idea to look up changelings on the tablet. I didn't know she could type."

The tote bag toppled over. Necklaces tumbled out everywhere, along with two nature faeries landing on their bottoms. Chaos snuck over the top of Timmy's shoulder. She pointed and then flew down and snagged Timmy's necklace.

"Hey," Timmy said.

"Yes, Chaos," Nan said, "we can see they're the same." Nan turned to Carissa. "That's what gave her the idea of the protection for the house. She's clever."

"Clever but causing trouble, like always." Carissa took a sip and then set down the tea. She asked Timmy, "Shouldn't you be getting home? Your parents will be worried about you."

Carissa glanced at the digital clock on the bookshelf: 4:00 p.m. The school bus had to have dropped him off at least half an hour ago.

"They're at a meeting, business association or something. They won't be back for at least another ten minutes."

"Well, then, Gilly will be waiting to watch over you."

"No, they said this morning that when school got out, I should just wait for them to get home."

"What, all alone? With so many neighbors on the street to care for you?" Nan asked.

"I'm big enough now to be home by myself. That's what they said this morning, and it's only a half hour."

Carissa looked at Nan, who shook her head. The Harbridges weren't ones to pay much mind to events in Moss Hill, except when it concerned their business. Even they had to be aware of the unseelie and the rumors of the evil fae targeting their island town. Would they really leave their eight-year-old home alone, even for just a half hour, instead of merely asking a neighbor to look after him? Perhaps they didn't trust their neighbors. Could they have heard about the changeling rumor and decided it was true?

"Timmy, you can't tell anyone about the changelings—not yet."

"But why? There's all sorts of information in the fae archives. These changelings are dangerous. We've got to warn people."

Chaos sat on his shoulder as if to agree. Carissa found it hard to combat his logic, but he was too young to be involved in this fight.

"We don't know for sure yet if that's what they are, and warning people can easily frighten them. There's an order to things. We have to know what we're dealing with first, then tell the sidhe guard, then—"

"But then it'll be too late!" Timmy stood up, balling his fists.

Chaos nearly fell from his quick action, but when she saw what he was doing, she mimicked his expression.

"Timmy, you don't understand, you could get hurt," Carissa began.

"People are already getting hurt!" Timmy's shouting was followed by waving fists from Chaos and frozen faces for Hiya and Cynth. Carissa tried to interject once more, but it only increased his volume. "I told you my schoolmates were acting funny! They've been taken—"

"All right, calm down, everyone," Nan said. "Think of it this way, Tim. If you say that there are changelings and there aren't, then you lose people's trust. If you say that there are changelings and there really are, then they know you're on to them. Best keep your eyes open and report back to us anything unusual."

"Like...a spy?" Timmy was still breathing hard, but he'd calmed enough to at least think about Nan's words.

"Exactly," Nan said.

She pointed to his necklace. "And keep that charm. A spy has to stay safe above all, or else how will we defeat the changelings?"

Carissa smiled at Nan's wisdom. Timmy accepted his "mission." Picking up a handful of charms, Carissa handed them to Timmy.

"Here," she said, "for your friends. But remember, telling the other children might put them in danger. Don't confront any of the ones you think are changelings." She turned to Nan. "Holly and I told Maren our theory. They went after the changeling, and I don't know what's happened to them." She was genuinely worried about that and showed it, just enough for Timmy to understand how serious things stood at the moment. "Just keep watch at school, but nothing else, okay? Promise me?"

Timmy's lips pulled aside in thought. Finally, he nodded. "Okay, promise."

# Chapter 9

## Like a Charm

Timmy hurried home at the sound of his parents' car pulling into their driveway. Carissa watched him from the window with a nagging worry that he would put himself in danger. If he were like everyone else in Moss Hill, he'd let his knowledge of the changelings slip and attract the wrong sort of attention.

Cari tried to let the feeling go. Timmy wasn't like everyone else in Moss Hill. He was brighter than his parents realized, more so even than Carissa had estimated. He would be fine. But would Maren? Carissa glanced at her phone. It wasn't like Maren to miss a message.

"Chaos," Carissa said sharply.

Her eyes searched the room for the sprite. The nature faerie shook at the sound, fluttering to safety at Nan's shoulder. Once perched there, she launched into a silent rant about how unfair Carissa was for being mad at her. In the six months she'd been with Cari and Nan, Chaos's sign language had become clear enough for both of them to understand. She was going so fast now, Carissa could hardly keep up, but still, she made out enough to get the gist that Chaos was just doing the job Mrs. Corvus had sent her here to do: protect Moss Hill from unseelie faeries. Carissa had never met Mrs. Corvus, but

Chaos liked to use her as an excuse not to listen to Cari sometimes.

"Oh, hush, Chaos, you're shouting in my ear," Nan said.

The sign language wasn't exactly shouting, but nature faeries did make a sort of jingling sound when they were emotional. Even Hiya and Cynth, whom Carissa suspected didn't really understand what was going on, were upset. The siblings never held hands otherwise.

"Sorry," Carissa put her hands up to calm Chaos down, "I'm not mad, really, I just need you to do something for me."

Chaos stopped, narrowed her eyes and then crossed her arms. She lifted her chin and one eyebrow as if to say: "I'm listening."

Carissa put a hand on her hip with equal attitude. "Summon Alden. He, Holly, and Maren were tracking a changeling, and I can't contact any of them. I've never seen Alden ignore your call, Chaos, please, will you summon him?"

Chaos straightened. She flew above high above the couch, pointing to the empty space in the center of the room. Closing her eyes, Chaos shot faerie dust from her hands and a red light swirled before them. The light surged into not one form, but three. A confused bean tighe, a stunned human, and a shadow-like ankou materialized in front of them. Carissa's jaw dropped. Chaos wasn't just summoning Alden, she was—

"Who shifted us?" Holly demanded.

"We're in Cari's house," Maren marveled. To Holly, she added, "I told you it was Cari calling. If you would have just let me answer—"

A shadowy figure caught Maren's eye. Alden quickly transformed from black shadow to skeleton to human form. Chaos fluttered to his shoulder. She appeared happy as ever to see him. Maren's face lost its color.

"You!" Holly shouted. "I knew you were following us."

"It's you," Maren touched her head like it was spinning, "the ankou." She turned on Holly. "You knew a Grim Reaper was following us and you didn't think to mention it?"

Alden looked at Carissa as if silently asking her to make this stop.

Holly shuffled through her purse and took out a black potion, aiming it for Alden's head.

"Hide thee, ank—"

"No!" Carissa grabbed Holly's wrist. "He's a friend."

Holly seemed unconvinced but eventually relaxed her hand. Carissa let go. Nan rose from the sofa, taking the teapot with her, and walked past the lot of them.

"I think I ought to put on another kettle. C'mon, Hiya, Cynth, help me with the tea."

The two faeries looked between her and the rest of the group. Scratching her head, Cynth shrugged and pointed toward the hallway, telling Hiya to go ahead and follow Nan. She did the same.

Holly turned her attention to Chaos, knowing somehow that it was she who'd shifted them.

"I ought to tell Mrs. Corvus on you, naughty fairy. We were so close to catching her."

"Tabitha?" Carissa asked.

"The changeling," Maren said.

Holly elaborated, "We caught up with her on Elderberry Road. Would've caught her, too, except someone shifted us from there to here."

"You wouldn't have caught her," Alden said.

Holly huffed. "Of course we would have."

"Maybe not," Maren said. "You weren't there to collect us, were you?"

She paled and backed away from Alden. He sighed, looking at Carissa again. Taking this as a cue, Cari put an arm around Maren.

"He doesn't mean it like that."

Alden pointed at Holly. "On Fourth Street, you were going to use a pink potion. It was rosehip, based on the look of it."

Chaos was nodding as if she knew what he was going to say.

"That's right," Holly's eyebrow raised, seemingly waiting for more information.

"Against one changeling it might've been enough to put it to sleep, but if it was leading you into a trap…."

"You mean there's more than one changeling?" Maren asked.

She seemed to be losing some of her ability to stand. Carissa gestured to the couch for them to all have a seat while finding her own place on a sofa chair. Nan came back with the tea and some crumpets on a tray. That was so like Nan. They were talking about a changeling invasion, and she was serving sweets. And how like Chaos to fly down and claim one for herself before Nan had even set the tray down.

"They're for the guests, Chaos." Nan's reprimand fell on deaf ears.

Chaos chomped happily while Carissa explained about Timmy and the few strange customers who had visited the shop. Alden continued with his reasoning as to why he'd felt the changeling was leading them into a trap.

"It was heading deeper into the town, not away from humans like you'd expect a caught faerie to do. Whenever you lost the trail, you'd picked it up again in a few minutes. It was as if it wanted you to follow. I don't know if there are other changelings about, but if there are any, one of them can attack while you're distracted. You'll need a stronger potion and some sort of protection on yourself so they can't switch places with you first."

"Cari made some charms," Maren offered.

Chaos snapped out of her crumpet rampage long enough to use her magic on a charm necklace. It floated in the air while the nature faerie went back to her food. Carissa snatched it and held it in an open palm for the room to see.

"It was for the children," Cari said. "I'm not sure it's enough, though."

"To ward off an individual changeling, it should be enough. Especially if all the children are wearing them. But if we're facing off with a group of them, we'll need a few more ingredients and some combined magical power."

Holly tapped her bag. "I have more than enough magic to face a group of changelings, and I daresay I know a trick or two for catching fae, since I am one myself."

"With respect—" Alden finally sat in a chair. If he was attempting to lower himself to Holly's eye level, he still had a long way to go. "Changelings target humans, not other fae. Druids know more about this than faeries."

"What would an ankou know about druids?" Holly asked. Carissa had never seen an eyebrow used to drop a gauntlet, but the way Holly's brow raised and fell with conviction was the most direct unspoken challenge she'd ever seen.

Holly held her head high and her shoulders straight. In the short time she'd known her, Carissa could see that Holly was a proud faerie, but never so much as now, when someone dared to question her magical knowledge. No doubt no ankou had ever had more knowledge than a bean tighe who's been in the direct service of a Tuatha de Danann, but Alden wasn't just an ankou.

"Forgive me if I overstepped," Alden said, humble as always, "but before my death, I was trained by the Morrigan in druidic magic."

Holly's eyes widened and she plopped on the couch.

"Of course," she whispered. "You're Jane's brother." Her face reddened, and she put a hand to her lips, uttering an embarrassed laugh. "Silly and old. I am that sometimes…oh, but if Macara hadn't dashed off and just told me there was already a protector in Moss Hill—sorry, Carissa, I mean an experienced one—well, that changes things."

Carissa knew she only meant well, but Holly's words hurt. Her take-charge attitude had apparently been because she didn't think that Carissa had enough magical knowledge to protect the island. She was right, of course. But that's precisely why it hurt.

Alden put a hand to his temple, which Carissa had come to know was his way of showing frustration. "The problem now is that the changeling disappeared into the men-an-tols."

"The what?" Carissa asked.

He looked at her. "The baby came back, didn't she?"

All three looked at Carissa, who nodded despite the confusion scribbled on her face.

She asked again, "What's a men-a-tol?"

"The old rocks in the park on First Street and Elderberry."

Carissa opened her mouth to restate her confusion, but then it dawned on her which ones Maren was talking about. "The stones with the circular holes in them? The ones by the school?"

"They're portals," Holly explained.

"The changeling used one of them to escape," Alden said. He turned his head to Holly. "And there's no way to track a fae once they've gone through."

"How can the stones be portals? We used to jump through those all the time as children. No one ever transported anywhere," Carissa challenged.

"They only work if you're tied to someone through binding magic. The magic will switch places with you," Holly said.

"But Alayna was back in her crib. How did she get there if the men-a-tol just switches places with the changeling?" Carissa asked.

Alden raised a hand. "That was me. I brought the baby to her parents."

"Teleportation. I'll never get used to knowing an ankou," Maren remarked.

"So, theoretically, we could use the men-a-tols to switch out all the changelings," Carissa said.

"Good luck getting them all to line up for you," Holly said.

Alden added, "The men-a-tol magic is ancient and it would work. There are other stones like it. One in Cornwall called the Crick Stone. The makers didn't just create the larger stones. There are smaller ones that help you see a changeling—"

"Adder stones," Holly said. "Oh, why didn't I think of that?" She put a hand to her head.

Alden shrugged. "It's not faerie magic. It's druidic. That's why you need a druid's help on this."

"Wait, what do you mean smaller ones help you see changelings?" Carissa asked.

Holly was the one who answered. "Old druids used them to see faeries of all sorts, but they're especially useful with changelings."

"So, do you have one?" Maren asked, picking up her tea for the first time.

Holly looked at Alden, who shook his head.

"I know how to make one in theory, but…." He looked at his hands.

The flesh turned to skeleton before their eyes and changed back again. Carissa felt a chill in her bones, and Maren's cup rattled on its saucer. Chaos clung to Alden in sympathy.

"Right," Holly said, "you're not a druid anymore—not a live one, anyway. You can't make one. But your sister can."

"She can make potions, too. Ones that expose the trolls and ones that can immobilize them. It'll take time," Alden said.

"How much time?" Cari asked.

"A day or two," Alden answered.

"Then we've not a moment to waste," Holly insisted. "Your sister can make the items. You and I can help her." She popped up from the sofa. "Come on."

"What about your parents? Won't they be surprised if you show up at your house?" Carissa asked.

Holly answered for Alden. "They're away on business. They seem to be doing that a lot lately."

Maren set down her tea. "What can Carissa and I do?"

"I'm afraid a human won't be of much help," Holly said, "but you're welcome to come with us."

Carissa winced. If Holly only knew how that would infuriate Maren, who'd been feeling left out. Just the way

Maren breathed in that long, slow exhale like a fire-breathing dragon, showed her ire.

"I can't," Carissa said. "I have a date with Cameron." Then, because she felt selfish for not helping, she added, "He's been helping with the case. Maybe he's found something that could be helpful."

Carissa hoped Alden and Holly hadn't been disappointed by her choosing a date over the safety of Moss Hill. She had to see Cam. She knew how important this date was to him and, if she was honest, she was really looking forward to their first Valentine's together, too. Besides, maybe he had some insight into what was going on. Carissa only hoped Maren had plans of her own tonight, since she knew this wasn't a night she would want to be alone.

"I'm not going to sit around and do nothing," Maren countered. She sprang to her feet and turned to Alden. "I'm sure I can help somehow."

Before Holly could shake her head or Alden could shrug, Nan, who'd been uncharacteristically quiet up to this point, spoke.

"Maybe there is something we humans can do," Nan reasoned. "In fact, I think I ought to have already done this before, but I lacked the courage. Perhaps you can help."

Holly and Alden both turned their heads. The bean tighe had a way of using her right eyebrow as a language in and of itself. This time she raised it into an unspoken question only Nan seemed to decipher.

Nan gave a solemn nod, and that was that. The exchange wasn't missed by the ankou or by Carissa, who shared a confused glance of their own. Then, Alden took Holly's hand and tilted his head to Chaos.

"Are you coming too?" he asked.

"She'd better not," Carissa said, earning her a sharp look from Chaos. Carissa matched Chaos's ire with a look of her own and sternly replied, "You were the one who said you wanted to be there for Cam's surprise, remember?"

Chaos waved a hand and crossed her arms. That's boring, is what she meant. Sure, it was boring now that she had a chance to chase changelings.

"Actually, I could use your help, too, Chaos," Nan said. "You might be glad you stayed."

Again, Alden's line of sight shifted to Cari, the mutual question played across both their faces. Nan was acting odd, and she wasn't subtle about it. The only one who wasn't noticing was Maren, who just seemed glad to be chosen for something. She sat with her chin up, not looking as Holly took Alden's arm and the two of them disappeared.

Chaos made a beeline to Nan's shoulder like she was the most intriguing person in the room. Nan stood. Maren sprang to her feet and voice rose in excitement. She may have noticed something in Nan's tone, but her mind seemed to have immediately provided an answer.

"So, what are we doing? A potion or something to add to the charms?"

Nan responded by loading the tray with the teacups and saucers, then she walked into the kitchen. Carissa and Maren followed.

"I knew it! It's a potion, isn't it?" Maren asked. "I'm getting good at recipes, I could bake it right into something—like cookies. The changelings would never know."

"Maren, my dear," Nan said, setting the tray by the sink, "you'll never know what's going on if you keep talking."

"Right, sorry," Maren said as she tucked a stray lock of hair behind her ear.

Once Nan was satisfied that she would use that ear to listen, she spoke.

"How many rooms are in this house?" Nan directed her question to Carissa.

The only response Cari could think of was to check Nan's forehead and wonder if one hundred and seventy years was the point past which a longevity spell could protect against dementia. That wasn't the course of action she opted for, though. Instead, she closed her jutting jaw and opened it again to answer.

"Yours, mine, the kitchen, and the living room. That's four."

Nan pointed up at the ceiling but didn't look up.

"There's only one room in the whole upstairs?" she asked, as if challenging her granddaughter's logic about the rooms in her own home.

Carissa almost responded that it was the master, so of course, it occupied more space. But mid-reply, Maren answered for her.

"And your grandfather's study." Maren pointed it out as if it were evident.

Carissa's forehead creased.

"The study," she said, almost to herself. She vaguely recalled that such a room existed but couldn't picture it at all. Had she ever even been in it or did she just remember it from the floor plan? Her fingers tapped her temple as if she could press a button to restore the memory. "How could I forget Grandfather's study?"

"It's not very memorable." Maren shrugged. "Just old books and things."

Carissa turned to Maren. "How do you know about it?" More specifically, she wondered how Maren could know about it when she didn't.

"It's a magically sealed room," Nan explained. "The more you think about the room, the more it shuts you out. The best way to wander into it is by not thinking."

Nan and Carissa looked at Maren. She caught on enough to be offended. Maren immediately put her hand on her hips.

"You make it sound like I don't ever use my mind."

Chaos flew over and patted Maren's shoulder while Nan reassured her. "You use your mind as much as your ears: sometimes too much and other times not at all. That is to say: you're human." She turned to Carissa. "And that's the key of it. Even if you do know that it's there, Cari, you won't ever be let inside. It's designed to keep fae and nosy humans out."

"Then why did it let Maren in?" Carissa asked.

"I'm really trying not to be offended here," Maren said, crossing her arms.

"Sorry," Carissa said, "but I mean, if you were curious about it, why would it let you in?"

"I wasn't curious about it," Maren explained. "It's just a study full of old things. The most I ever wondered about it was why you didn't convert it into an office of your own."

Nan laughed. "'A study full of old things' is hardly something to find dull. It should be the most curious thing in the world. Leave it to a young person to underestimate the value of 'old things.'"

Nan walked past them, leading the way upstairs. Maren followed next while Carissa lagged behind. Cari, who traveled these steps daily, felt she was venturing into new territory. She'd discovered in the last few months that Nan had secrets. By extension, so did her parents, since the secrets all culminated into one: Carissa's grandfather was a descendant of a Tuatha de Danann. It wasn't just any Tuatha de Danann, but Maeve, the warrior queen of Connaught. Carissa had read about her since her grandmother's revelation and had been horrified to learn that she was revered by the unseelie. Evil faeries aside, Maeve was a powerful figure and a black mark in her family history. Carissa hadn't found the courage yet to tell Cameron or Maren about her.

Truthfully, she was still making sense of the information herself. As they made it to the top landing and turned right, Carissa realized that knowledge might just have scratched the surface. The corner of the house was deeper than Cari had noticed before.

This was especially true of the wooden door with the gold knob that she passed by every day. She had always known it was there, but her eyes skirted over it, much like what they were doing now.

"What are we doing up here?" Maren asked.

She looked puzzled. How could she forget? Carissa almost laughed at the absurdity. Then, she forgot too. Why were they up here? It was something to do with a room. She turned her head, looking at her bedroom. Were they looking for something in there?

A flash of faerie dust clouded her sight and Chaos's little fingers pushed at Carissa's chin, turning her back. Carissa coughed and swatted at the faerie.

"Chaos! What on earth are you doing?"

The little faerie rammed into her back, pushing her farther and farther away from her room.

"Quit it!" Carissa said.

"She can't," Nan said. "Listen to her. She has something to show you."

"Then we should follow her," Maren added.

Carissa had no choice since Chaos was using all her faerie strength to push her along.

"All right! I'm going." Carissa came face to face with a door, or rather crashed into it, and felt a shock the moment her hand found the handle. "Ouch!" she said, pulling back and cradling her fingers.

"What's wrong?" Maren asked.

Chaos signed furiously, but Carissa couldn't make out what she was saying. Nan could. Or maybe she already knew before Chaos said a word.

"The study is designed to keep you out, Carissa, because you have the kind of magic that can open it."

Cari shook her head.

"I don't know how," she said.

Chaos tugged at her hand, pulling it toward the door until it was flat against the wood. The magic stung. Carissa wanted to pull away again, but Chaos wouldn't let her. Instead, the sprite held her tiny hands firmly on top of hers. Despite her size, the nature faerie burst with enough magic to swirl around Carissa's fingers.

Carissa felt the power behind it as if it were calling her own magic forth. How could that be? Carissa had little time to wonder since she felt more than elf-light pumping through her veins now. Whatever power she was using, it was stronger than any she'd used before.

The door glowed, radiantly, then blindingly so that Carissa had to look away. A sudden flash and then it was over. By the time the light had gone, Cari had found that the door had opened.

Chaos floated to Cari's shoulder, clearly exhausted. Carissa took a step through the open door, and Maren and Nan followed.

The room, which to Carissa's knowledge she had never seen before, reminded her somewhat of her father's study in their cottage in Vale. The dark wood bookcases seemed to have grown from the walls at every angle and were filled to the brim with massive tomes. Among the volumes were old treasure boxes and trinkets whose significance Carissa neither knew nor understood.

"See? It's just a study," Maren said. She picked up a book and paged through it. "There's nothing even written on these pages. It's just a journal."

"Let me see."

Carissa held out her hand. Maren gave her the book and continued looking through the shelves for something more interesting. When Carissa opened the book, she immediately looked up at Nan, who smiled.

"Yes, you can read it. We can't. Faerie eyes only," Nan said.

This caught Maren's attention. She walked up to them.

"You mean there's something written in that book?"

"Not just something," Carissa answered. "Everything." She pointed to where there would be a title: *The Complete Compendium of Magic and Myth.*

"Amazing," Maren remarked.

"Not the word I was thinking of," Carissa said.

"Wonderful? Fantastic?" Maren offered as she wandered around the room.

"Deceitful," Cari replied. She turned to Nan. "Why didn't you tell me about this room before? Did my parents know about this room? Do you know how many times I could've used this knowledge?"

Nan held up a hand. "I was told never to open this room, especially not to you."

"Why?" Maren asked.

"Who told you that?" Carissa asked.

"Your grandfather," Nan answered. To Maren, she added, "Because opening it requires a type of magic that would be felt by the unseelie. It would reveal your presence to them and draw them to Moss Hill."

Carissa knew what type of magic her grandmother meant. Macara had given her the same warning when she'd left. She'd said that the magic of a Tuatha de Danann was powerful enough to be felt by the fae and that Cari's magic, in particular, might be felt by the unseelie. Whether it was because she was inexperienced with that magic or because it was related to Maeve's magical legacy, was unclear. Still, it begged a question:

"Why let me open it now?"

"The unseelie have already invaded Moss Hill. They're all over this island. If you can't get them off this island, no one else will be able to," Nan explained.

"Desperate times," Maren chimed in.

A low rumbling stole their attention. All three of them looked to the desk, where Chaos hovered atop the left side. Carissa walked around it, eyes focused on where Chaos was pointing. The sprite's magical energy caused the desk drawer to quiver in place. With a little help from Cari, in the form of more of the mysterious magic that was not her elf-light, the desk drawer slid open.

Chaos dove in. Carissa didn't have to wonder what she was after. She could see it plain as day. Chaos zipped up with a twirl, holding the object over her head like a trophy.

It was a gray stone, with a nearly perfect circle cut out of the middle.

"Is that…?" Maren asked.

"An adder stone," Nan replied.

"Desperate measures," Carissa said, sharing a look with Chaos.

# Chapter 10

## Date with Destiny

Time ran away from Carissa about as fast as the changeling had from Holly. She, Chaos, and Maren scoured the items in her grandfather's study for at least an hour. Finally taking in the fact that Carissa was part of an ancient race more powerful than any on earth, Maren began asking a series of unrelenting questions.

"So, you're Tuatha de Danaan, elf, and human. And you're always saying you don't know how to use magic very well?"

Carissa shrugged. "I wasn't trained."

"But your dad taught you some of the elf-light. I've seen you use it. It looks just like your dad's magic."

"What I use is elf-magic," Cari explained. "I've never knowingly used the Tuatha de Danaan magic."

Maren pointed to the giant book currently open in her lap. "It says here that Tuatha de Danaan magic takes on its form according to the personality. With some people, it comes out purple, some blue or green, some like smoke, some dust, some lightning. It's a bit confusing."

"Your grandfather's was orange. It was like that hue in the sky just before sunset." Nan stared off into the distance with a nostalgic look. It made Cari wish she'd had a chance to know her grandfather before he'd died.

Maren asked, "Do they control it? Or does it just come out like it does? I mean, what if Cari's looks just like elf-light?"

"With Gareth, it was his favorite color. I'm not sure about other Tuatha de Danaan. I suppose it could be anything that causes it to take form as it does," Nan explained.

"I wonder if it's something you choose," Carissa added.

Chaos practiced with poofs of faerie dust all over the shelves. The colors varied to some extent, but each glitter puff was somewhat multicolored. She kept trying, disregarding the warning looks from Carissa.

"If I had a choice, mine would be pink," Maren announced. She looked at Cari. "Just for fun, when you're using your power for the first time, just think pink and see what happens."

"I don't think the color is all that important, Maren." Carissa smiled.

"Don't you have a date tonight?" Nan interrupted.

"What time is it? I completely forgot!" Carissa pulled her phone out of her pocket.

Chaos flew through the air, making a heart-shaped trail of mostly pink faerie dust around Carissa's face. In cartoons it was cute, in real life it was annoying. Carissa batted away the glittery magic, jumped from the pile of books and artifacts she and Maren had piled on the floor, and furiously tapped against the screen of her phone.

"I'd better tell Cam not to hurry. He's going to be upset that I'm late." She was mostly talking to herself, but Maren had to add her two cents.

"You don't want to be late for tonight. Cameron has everything planned out perfectly. It's going to be such a special Valentine's Day!"

Carissa's hand hovered before pressing the button to call Cam. She looked up, studying Maren's mysterious expression.

"A special Valentine's Day?"

She knew he had plans for tonight, but Maren was acting like there was something more to it. Now that she thought about it, Cam had made a big deal of it too. Carissa pressed the home button and set the phone on the desk. All she had to do was cross her arms and give Maren that angry elf look, and her friend put her hands up.

"Forget I said anything. It's supposed to be a secret."

Maren put a hand to her mouth, zipping it up and throwing a pretend key away like she'd done as a schoolgirl when she swore she wouldn't tell a secret.

"You know something," Carissa accused, "spill it."

"Cam is going to ask you...." Maren's mouth was clamped shut. Her eyes moved down to where both of Chaos's hands were holding her mouth closed. Slowly, the startled woman raised one brow. As her lips parted, Chaos's hands drew back, sparkling with magic. Maren didn't understand nature faerie gestures, but she could recognize a threat when she saw one.

"Chaos! You know too?" Carissa pointed at the sprite. "You tell me, right now."

Chaos let go of Maren, but only to wag a finger and shake her head. Carissa stood there with her mouth agape, wondering what they weren't saying.

He couldn't be asking her to move in. People in Moss Hill were a little old-fashioned for that. Could he be proposing? No, that couldn't be it. They hadn't even been dating for two months.

"What is he going to ask me?" Carissa practically shouted out of sheer frustration.

Nan, who'd been sitting at the desk, rasped on the table for Carissa's attention. "Why don't you call him and ask?"

Carissa's shoulders fell as she picked up her phone. "I can't just ask. He's got it all planned, apparently."

"Then why don't you stop asking and let things go as planned?" She said it calmly, but Carissa knew that this was Nan's way of chiding her.

She sighed. "Point taken." She scrolled through her phone to find Cam's number.

"Good," Nan said. "I'll make dinner. Maren, are you staying?"

Maren shrugged. "I don't have anywhere else to be."

The sentiment stung. Carissa had been frantic over a possible proposal while her friend had only a possible boyfriend who wasn't even on the island for Valentine's Day. She ought to just be grateful to have Cam in her life. Whatever he was going to ask, she'd have to cross that bridge when she came to it.

Nan and Maren left the room all cluttered, overlooking the giant mess by the desk.

Carissa's phone rang while Chaos settled on her ear. The sprite's hand touched the side of her neck. Rather than a gesture of comfort, it was more likely the best position for Chaos to eavesdrop.

"Hello?" Cameron's distracted voice said.

"Hey, Cam." Carissa tried for as light a tone as possible. "I'm running a little late. I hope you aren't on your way yet."

"On my way?" he asked.

Carissa's eyebrows crinkled. Did he really not know what she was talking about?

"For our date," she said.

"Date? Oh, right, our date. Of course, no I got held up at the office." He lowered his voice. "Did you know there's a changeling on the loose?"

"Yes!" she said a little too quickly, and loudly enough to earn a swat on her neck from Chaos's little hand. "I told you about it earlier." She couldn't believe she had to remind him.

"You did?" he asked.

Well, no. Carissa hadn't told him about a changeling being on the loose. She hadn't even used the word "changeling" because she'd wanted to avoid panic in the town. This was what happened when she held back from the people around her. She needed to stop doing that.

"Never mind," she said, both to silence the voice in her head scolding her for her closed nature, and to keep from confusing Cam more. "Did you find out about Mrs. O'Mally? And did you check on Tabitha?"

"Tabitha?" he asked.

"Yes, you were going into Vale. I asked you to get Varick to check on Tabitha."

"Oh, right," he sounded exhausted. "I'm sorry, it slipped my mind. I didn't even get to Vale today. I'll have to go tomorrow."

"It's okay," Carissa said, hoping that it was, in fact, okay.

Briefly, she pictured the angry mothers storming Tabitha's house, but she pushed the image away. If Cam hadn't known about Tabitha, then no one had brought it up in the town hall. That was a good sign.

They were panicking about a changeling on the loose, though, which meant Holly's wild chase through town had been witnessed. At least they weren't also talking about an ankou, so Alden had stayed hidden well enough. She didn't want to imagine what the panic would have been like if the Mossies had seen him.

Still, in light of all this changeling business, she wondered if a Valentine date was appropriate. Wouldn't their time be better spent in search of the changeling? She bit her lip, thinking about this question Cam was going to ask her. All the more reason to cancel.

"Cam, I know you had big plans for tonight, but maybe we should keep working on finding the changeling."

"No," Cameron said quickly enough to cause Carissa's elf ears to twitch. His pace slowed to normal. "It's Valentine's Day. Plus, you have to eat dinner, don't you?"

Carissa's hand traveled to her waist. Her stomach ached, but she wasn't sure if it was nerves or hunger.

"All right," she gave in, "but if you're still at the office—"

"I'm not, sorry. I'm on an errand. I'll be over soon," he said and abruptly hung up.

Carissa blinked, pulled her phone away from her ear to give it a glance, and looked at Chaos when the screen went black. Chaos hovered beside her with as confused an expression.

"That was strange," Carissa said to herself.

The sprite nodded. Cameron had never just hung up on her before. Perhaps it was only stress from the office.

"Well, I guess I should get ready," Carissa remarked.

Chaos floated over the desk to where the adder stone was sitting on top of a pile of books. She heaved the stoned up and carried it into Carissa's open palm.

"Good thinking," Carissa praised. "Better take this with me, just in case."

***

CAMERON WAS NOT HIMSELF. Camera Cam was full-on tonight, from his flashy smile to the shiny shoes. He arrived at her doorstep right on time with a handful of fresh-cut roses and a neatly pressed suit. He'd even come with a chauffeur of his own. Being ambassador to Vale had its perks, but Carissa wasn't sure she liked this one. The presence of the driver only made her self-conscious during the ride. Cameron filled the car with enough empty talk and humor for both of them.

"Are you okay?" Cam finally asked.

Carissa gave a half-hearted smile. "Fine." She fell noticeably short of cheery, but then Cameron's joviality was over the top. She didn't want to spoil the mood, but she couldn't pretend everything was all right. She tried a more honest reaction. "Sorry, there's just a lot on my mind right now."

"Oh? Like what?" Cam asked.

For one, Hiya and Cynth kept pretend sword-fighting with two of the roses Cam had brought. She'd put the flowers in a vase, but they'd insisted on bringing two along, promising they'd only hold them. That lasted about a minute. Chaos, who had not brought a flower, had finally had enough of the shenanigans and used her faerie magic to lift the bulbs to the car's roof. The nature faeries, still clinging to them, clashed right into each other. This caused a whole new fight of its own, in which Carissa had to intervene.

"Cut it out, you three. I didn't bring you along to fight."

She hadn't brought them along at all. It was Chaos who'd insisted on coming to protect Carissa—should any changelings show up to dinner. Once Chaos had made up her mind, that was that. Hiya and Cynth were just as stubborn. They knew about Cameron and Carissa's date, and so they'd shown up on the doorstep right when he'd arrived. It was almost as if they had it planned.

The three sprites sat quietly for about one more minute before the car came to a stop. Carissa made to open her own door, but Cam put a hand on her arm as a silent signal to wait. She smiled as he swung around the back of the car and opened her door for her. The perfect gentleman, he offered his hand. She gratefully took it and exited the vehicle.

Hiya made the same type of motion to Chaos and Cynth, holding out both his hands for the girl faeries, but it was more of a parody than an actual gesture. It earned him a swat on the hand from Cynth and an eye roll from Chaos. Carissa ignored the antics as they walked into the restaurant.

"The Rose Garden?" Her eyes widened.

She looked at Cam. He only grinned like a cartoon caricature of himself as he nodded a "thank you" to the doorman. He wasn't sparing any expense.

The restaurant off the side of the Failte Hotel had always been high-brow. Since the renovations, it had become even more so, with only more affluent residents and guests able to afford the cost.

"I can't believe you reserved a table here," Carissa whispered as they were ushered to seats right near a window.

"Anything for you," Cam said as he pulled out a chair for her to sit.

The waiter handed them their menus and took their drink orders. Cam ordered red wine for the occasion—the finest the restaurant had to order. The night should have been perfect. Especially since everything seemed to be going so smoothly.

Hiya and Cynth pointed to a young couple whose small children were coloring heart-shaped papers. The waiter did not have to be versed in nature faerie to pick up the hint. He promised to bring them the same heart-shaped paper and crayons before leaving the table.

It was a good thing he came back with the drinks and distraction because without the coloring paper, the sprites zipped through the hall like nosy neighbors. They sat on the shoulder of a young girl coloring with a pink crayon. The child giggled upon noticing the faeries. Carissa noted the pendant around the girl's neck and smiled, happy that some children in Moss Hill were already protected.

"Hiya, Cynth!" Carissa called them back. She pointed at the corner of the table by the bread basket. "Stay out of sight. There might be tourists around here tonight, and you don't want them to see you."

"So," Cam began the moment they'd placed their order, "you said you had a lot on your mind."

He flashed that goofy smile again. Didn't he realize the town was under threat? She asked him as much.

"You said there were reports to town hall about a changeling on the loose?"

He shrugged. "Sure, some people reported seeing it on Clover Street. It was being chased by a bean tighe." He seemed to think this was funny. His chuckle made Cari smile, genuinely, for the first time tonight.

"Holly." Carissa nodded. "She and Maren were chasing it."

"I would've liked to see that."

They both laughed. It felt good to laugh, but it only lasted a second. Then, Carissa remembered that Holly and Alden were working this very moment on finding a way to protect Moss Hill.

Carissa straightened up, leaning forward so that she could speak quietly enough for only Cam to hear. He cocked his head, amused at her sudden seriousness.

"There's more going on than one changeling," Carissa said.

"Really? What else?" He leaned forward too.

She filled him in on Tabitha, Mr. Crimbal, and the Cartwrights. This time, she tried not to leave anything out. The waiter interrupted them with their dinner before she had gotten the whole story out. At the end of it all, he whistled his disbelief.

"Wow. That is a lot to take in," he said.

"Holly's first thought was that it might be Tabitha, but she cooperated with us right away. I don't know. There are so many people involved: Mrs. O'Mally, Mr. Crimbal, Tabitha, even people at the Failte Abhaile. I think it's all related, but I can't figure out how."

"Then don't worry about it."

"What?" Carissa asked.

Even Chaos perked her tiny ears at Cam's statement. She stopped trying to get Hiya and Cynth to quit fighting over the purple crayon and wandered closer to Carissa. The snap of the crayon in two solved the problem anyway, but Chaos didn't seem to notice. She began rummaging through Carissa's purse. Carissa was too shocked by Cam's apathy to reprimand the sprite.

Cam shrugged. "You said yourself that Holly's got it all taken care of. Let her handle it."

"Cameron, this is serious. It could involve the whole town."

"I know. That's why it's not the right conversation for tonight." He took her hand. "Tonight is just about you and me."

Carissa couldn't believe what she was hearing. Moss Hill was everything to Cam. He wouldn't just ignore the safety of the town for the sake of a romantic night. Not even for Valentine's Day.

Maybe Cameron knew he'd upset her. Or perhaps he was just nervous. Whatever it was, almost as quickly as Cameron put his hand on top of hers, he snatched it back. Cam's fingers flew to the back of his neck the way they always did when he was nervous.

Carissa's stomach twisted, recalling Maren's cryptic statement. *Cam is going ask you....* What? What was he going to ask? She could only think of one thing that would make him act so strange.

She set down her fork and wiped her hands across the napkin on her lap.

"Cam, before you say anything else," she began, but Carissa trailed off as her eye caught the sight above Cameron's head.

There was Chaos heaving the adder stone up and peering down through it. What was she doing pointing it at Cam? More specifically, she was looking at the hand he was holding to his neck. A sudden realization dawned on her.

"Would you excuse me? I have to go to the restroom. I'll be right back," Carissa strung the words together like they were all part of the same sentence.

She got up before Cameron could say anything. Hiya and Cynth kept coloring away, pleased and oblivious as could be. Carissa's eyes shifted this way and that. Now she was either just being paranoid, or everyone in the restaurant seemed to be eyeing her through the corner of their eyes. Chaos hugged the adder stone, covering as much of it with her body as possible, and followed Carissa to the restroom. The half-elf moved as hastily as possible while still trying for a casual appearance.

In the restroom, she glanced at the bottoms of the stalls. They were empty. Making it back to the door, she twisted the lock.

"What did you see?" Cari whispered.

Chaos looked into the adder stone. Carissa took it from her hand.

"You saw something in the stone?"

Chaos nodded. Then, the sprite hunched forward, holding her arms up like claws. Either she saw a bear, or she was trying to determine whether Cam was some type of creature.

"A changeling?" Cari asked.

Again, the nature faerie nodded. Cameron was a changeling. Carissa felt her breath escape her like a blow to the heart. She clutched her forehead and closed her eyes. Of course, he was. Now that she thought about it, it had been evident since the last phone conversation. Why, oh why, hadn't she seen it?

She groaned. "I told him everything! Holly's plan, my grandfather's study, everything."

She felt dizzy. Chaos patted her head, and Carissa took a few breaths as her eyes fell on her reflection. *Get a hold of yourself,* she thought. She willed herself to calm down. Chaos looked into the mirror beside her. The nature faerie pointed to the stone.

"Right," she said. "All is not lost. We still have this and the necklaces."

There were still one or two facts she hadn't had time to accidentally spill. Now, all she had to do was get through dinner without giving anything else away. Maybe she could even turn the tables in her favor by adding in a misleading detail or two. She clutched the adder stone in her palm. Better yet, maybe this was her chance to catch a changeling.

# Chapter 11

## Flirting with Danger

Carissa came out of the restroom to a pair of ladies and the restaurant manager standing beside the door. She'd heard the knock but hadn't realized there were so many people behind it. Three pairs of eyes looked her up and down. The manager spoke.

"Is everything all right, miss?"

"Yes." Carissa noticed the frowns on the women's faces.

"The door is not supposed to be locked," the manager said.

His tone was level, but his face was angrier than was warranted. The blonde woman crossed her arms. The brunette did not. In fact, her hands hung awkwardly in white-knuckled fists. Was it her imagination, or were they cornering her against the door? The last thing Carissa needed was a scene. She tried stepping around them, but the brunette was unrelenting.

"Sorry," Carissa said. "I just needed a minute. It's all yours now."

The three of them stepped closer. Something was wrong. Cari got the distinct impression if she didn't make it out of the restaurant soon, she wasn't going to make it out at all. Chaos seemed to get the same feeling. A quick glance at the nature faerie showed two little fists ready for an attack. It would only be seconds before the three attackers noticed the faerie magic swirling at her hands.

Carissa looked behind the brunette, feigning a gasp. "What's the sidhe guard doing here?" she asked.

The brunette fell for it. Chaos unleashed her faerie dust in time for Carissa to sidestep the woman to her right. All three rubbed at their eyes. Dashing through the restaurant, she wished the sidhe guard really was there.

The restaurant was packed with customers. Several eyes shifted to her as she made it back to her table. It wasn't the whole restaurant, but enough to make her wonder just how many changelings there were in here. So much for catching a changeling. There were too many in here for her to take on alone.

Her heart was racing by the time she made it to her seat. She didn't sit down. Fake Cam stood up.

"Carissa? Is everything okay?" he asked.

Her mouth opened and closed. She couldn't think of a response. Her brain was screaming at her, but her heart was still seeing the man at the table as Cameron. She looked away just as the two nature faeries' eyes lifted from their coloring. In the background, a couple of heavy-set men stood up from the bar. They weren't even hiding the fact that they were looking right at her.

They weren't going to let her go so effortlessly. Somehow, she had to make her way past them without causing a scene. But she couldn't leave with Cam. His driver was probably a changeling, too.

Her eyes looked around for a way out. She spotted one familiar face: Mr. Greer, the librarian. Nan hadn't mentioned anything about anyone acting strangely at the library. He was probably still himself.

She watched him, ignoring Cameron as he asked her a second time if everything was all right.

Mr. Greer was saying goodbye to a man in a suit and a woman in a fancy dress. Carissa didn't recognize the couple. He was dressed in a suit and tie. Not a handsome man by nature, Declan Greer's brown hair frayed on the sides with a touch of grey. He was average in height and thin with enough style to his clothing to blend in with the crowd tonight. He shook hands with the man and kissed the woman on the cheek. As the couple left, he turned back to the table to pick up his coat. It was perfect timing.

"Carissa." Cam touched Cari's arm.

She jolted back, and the imposter pulled away. His sagging jaw and wide eyes gave a near convincing impression of concern. She almost believed it really was Cameron. Almost.

"Sorry," Carissa said. "I'm not feeling well. I think I need to leave."

"Sure, I'll get the check."

"No," she scooped her coat up and motioned with her fingers for Hiya and Cynth to get up.

The sprites moved slowly. Chaos rushed them along with a stern look and a few zaps of magic. They snuggled into her purse.

"You enjoy your meal. I don't want to spoil Valentine's Day for you."

"But you don't have a ride home." Cameron moved closer.

She stepped back. "Actually, I was going to see if Mr. Greer could give me a lift."

She raised her voice enough that Mr. Greer's head turned at the mention of his name. She caught his eye with a look as close to pleading as possible without raising suspicion. It worked. The librarian changed direction, walking to their table now.

"You're not making any sense, Cari," Cameron's voice lowered to a growl. "I don't have to finish my meal. Wait one minute, and I'll take you home." Cam took out his wallet and held up a hand to ask for the check.

"Hello, Carissa, Cam." The librarian had finally made it to the table.

Carissa greeted him while Cam stood by.

"Mr. Greer," Cari continued, "I wonder if you wouldn't mind giving me a ride. I'm not feeling well, and Cameron hasn't yet finished his meal."

Cameron physically pushed his way between them. "There's no need to trouble Mr. Greer. I'm perfectly able to take you home."

"I wasn't going toward Crescent Circle. I had some work to catch up on in the library. Sorry, Carissa," Mr. Greer said.

"That's okay." She took Mr. Greer's arm before he could argue, lying, "Nan was going to stop by there." Turning back to Cam, she added, "She can take me home from there."

"But—" the imposter argued.

Carissa acted as if she hadn't heard him, striking up a conversation with Mr. Greer as she pulled him out the door. She couldn't give the counterfeit Cam a chance to argue or Mr. Greer a chance to refuse.

"So, was it a special dinner tonight or just old friends?"

Mr. Greer scratched his head. "Um…neither. It was family that has just come into town."

"Oh? Are they staying at the Failte Abhaile?"

Carissa's eyes noted the waiter coming toward them. Her heart beat so that she could feel the elf-light pulsing through her blood. The hostess at the register moved in their direction. Carissa made a conscious effort to keep her magic from leaping through her fingertips. Both glared at her, but neither stopped them from leaving.

"Yes, they came in with the reunion."

The doorman met Carissa's eyes and glared. She clenched her jaw. A few more steps and she would be clear of the place.

"The reunion," she repeated absently, trying to be courteous to the man who was acting as her escape plan. They cleared the building and the next one. Then, her brain registered the words. "Which reunion?" she asked.

"A bunch of family and friends, they get together in different places around the world each year. The organizer was originally from Moss Hill, so she arranged it here this year."

"And they're family of yours?"

He nodded. "Some of them, yes."

She stopped and let go of Mr. Greer's arm. The old man took the opportunity to retrieve his car keys. She studied him while he did so. James Cartwright had suspected the visitors at the Failte Abhaile might be involved with the changelings. Was he hinting that he was a changeling, too?

He looked up at her with a quizzical expression. She was staring.

"The car is just a little farther," he said.

"That's all right, Mr. Greer. I just needed an excuse to leave."

His eyebrows knotted. "Is everything okay?"

He wasn't giving away any type of reaction. Maybe he didn't know about the changelings in the restaurant. Carissa smiled.

"Just some Valentine's troubles."

He nodded knowingly. "Glad I could help." He raised the hand that held the keys and said, "Goodnight," then he turned back. "You should be careful, though. I've heard there's trouble about."

He did know something. The look in his eyes had changed. It wasn't sneaky nor angry nor overly-humored. No, it was…regretful.

She watched him as he walked away. Now safe from changelings, Chaos took to the air. The other two nature faeries poked their noses up out of her new lavender bag. Hiya flinched when a figure appeared beside them, its shadow crossing over the bag.

A ghostly figure stepped right behind Carissa.

"You made it out safely?" the ankou asked.

Carissa turned to Alden. "Yes. Thanks for coming."

She had summoned Alden, or actually, Chaos had—to the ladies' restroom of all places. He could've transported them out right away, but there was no way she was leaving Hiya and Cynth in the hands of a changeling. She had to make it out of the restaurant herself, but once outside, she knew she'd be safe with the ankou around.

Well, almost. They still needed to be careful. Carissa pulled her locket out from her coat and twisted it. Stepping into the Otherworld, she joined Alden in a dark spot off the side of the building where it would be safe to watch others without being seen. Naturally, the nature faeries and ankou shifted with her to the Otherworld. She said her chant, seeing in both the human and faerie realms.

Carissa held her hand out to Chaos. The sprite knew what she wanted. Chaos used her magic to lift the adder stone from the purse.

"Does this work in the Otherworld?" Carissa asked Alden as she lifted it to her eye.

"Yes."

Cari gasped as she looked through it. First, to her left, Carissa caught Mr. Greer's form before he turned the corner. Then, to her right, she saw Cameron exiting the restaurant. The vision of each confirmed her worst fears. Pulling the stone away, she clutched it to her heart.

Cameron was definitely a changeling. The magic shimmered around him so that it created an unclear form. The adder stone made it glow but didn't settle on a clear image. That wasn't her only concern, though.

"Get Holly," she said to Alden. "We have a bigger problem than we thought."

That might've been an understatement. Changelings were one thing. What she'd seen was quite another.

Mr. Greer was a troll.

* * *

FOLLOWING CAM FELT WRONG. She knew it wasn't really Cam, but it looked like him, and she'd promised herself after the unwarranted jealousy with Tilly that she wouldn't be a distrustful type of girlfriend. This was different, naturally, but it still felt like spying.

With six people trailing one, it felt more like ganging up on a person than simple spying. True, three members of the group were nature faeries, but if anyone was going to give them away, it was the sprites. Alden had used his instant transport to bring Holly from the Everly's to where Carissa was trailing the changeling pretending to be Cameron.

Even though Carissa was hiding in the Otherworld, the fake Cam seemed paranoid, looking this way and that. Carissa expected the chauffeur to pick Cameron up, at which point it would be impossible to follow him on foot. The only way to catch him then would be to wait at Cameron's apartment, assuming he would go there. The impostor, however, did not call for the car. Instead, he walked by foot across the street and in the same direction as Mr. Greer.

The group could only watch from a distance. Crossing the road directly would mean taking the risk of being seen if the changeling could see into the Otherworld. Carissa passed the adder stone to Holly, who had a similar reaction to Carissa upon witnessing the true identities of Cam and Mr. Greer.

Even from across the street, it was clear that the two men were talking to each other. Carissa tried to concentrate. Elf ears could pick up sound better than a human's, though that distance was a challenge even for her.

Anything she could have heard was undermined by a distraction of three little sprites trying to get a view from their seats in the purse hanging from Carissa's shoulder. Hiya, not watching out for Cynth right in front of him, knocked into her accidentally, then purposely, as he pushed her out of his way. The two floated out of the purse, but, even then, they fought for a clear view. Cynth's reaction was to hit Hiya with faerie dust every time he got into her space. Chaos finally blasted them both, which only led to a full-on faerie dust fight.

"Stop," Carissa commanded. Then, seeing the shimmering mess all over her purse, she dropped her concentration entirely and tried swiping the dust off. "Look what you've done. You're ruining the new purse."

The faeries shrank back. Carissa's eyes traveled down to her shoes. More faerie dust covered the tips of the dressy mauve heels.

"Great, you've got my shoes, too."

Then she looked closer. It was a white powder, not the sparkled glitter of faerie dust. She had seen something like it before, back at the Seelie Tree.

"What's wrong?" Holly asked.

"Look." Carissa knelt down and swiped the dust onto her finger.

Holly grabbed Carissa's hand and pulled it close to her face. Then, she let go and began digging around in her oversized tote bag.

"Is it some type of faerie dust?" Carissa asked.

"Hold on," Holly said.

She pulled out a reddish-brown potion. Carissa couldn't make out exactly what the label said, but had the same mushroom smell and consistency as potion the bean tighe made in the shop. Carissa opened her mouth to ask Holly if it was the very same concoction when Holly unexpectedly poured the mix directly onto Cari's feet. A puff of smoke rose up from the powder in seconds. The pungent smell of rotten fungus filled her nose and mouth. She coughed, and the nature faeries gagged.

"Ugh! What is that?" Carissa asked.

"It's the mushroom mix." Holly wafted the foul air away with her hands.

"Why does it smell like that?" Carissa asked, waving her hands.

"It's a reaction to the troll dust."

"Troll dust?" Carissa stopped.

That made sense. Mr. Greer was a troll, maybe all the changelings in Moss Hill were trolls. That would mean that Tabitha was innocent. But did it mean that Mr. Greer or his family was guilty?

"He's moving," Alden said.

Cameron crossed the street again. Carissa moved back into the shadows so that he wouldn't see. She couldn't help whispering though.

"Should we grab him?"

Holly fiddled in her bag for another potion.

"There's a crowd," Alden said.

There was, in fact, a whole group of people coming out of the Rose Garden and walking in their direction. Were they human or fae? More specifically, were they changelings? Carissa tried the adder stone, but Holly nudged her. Cam was moving faster now.

Carissa and Holly kept to the shadows, but all of them continued following Cameron up the road. He walked two buildings down and turned into the Failte Abhaile Hotel. The lobby was lit up, and from what little they could see through the windows, the place was packed.

Carissa and the others stopped.

"I can't go in there," Alden said. "Someone there might recognize me."

"They might all be trolls, too," Holly pointed out.

"We can't get to him now," Carissa said, "but I know someone on the inside who might be able to help."

# Chapter 12

## Catch a Changeling

Confronting danger and chasing changelings left Carissa exhausted. Instead of any further investigating, she asked Alden to transport her home. Then, seeing that Nan was safe and Maren had returned to her own home, Carissa strengthened Chaos's protection spell over the house. She wasn't well-versed on the spells, but a thumbs up from the skilled nature faerie was enough for her to call it good.

She wished she could sleep, but worry about Cam filled her brain, so the best she could manage was a twilight sleep where images of changelings scared her awake every ten minutes. Around and around her mind went. The changelings were trolls, Tabitha was innocent, and Cameron was in danger.

The last thought began the cycle all over. The loop continued until the morning when she groggily prepared for work and ate breakfast in the early hours before Nan had even woken up. She scribbled out a note before leaving to remind her of their conversation last night.

"Don't go into work today. The library is not safe."

Nan had agreed last night. Mr. Greer might not be himself. She shuddered to think he could be a changeling. Or worse: he might be himself, but who he was might be a troll. No, it was better for Nan to stay in the magically protected home.

Cari stuck the note on the fridge and made it out the door without disturbing Nan or waking the nature faeries. Except for one. Chaos seemed in tune with Cari lately. Carissa didn't argue when she followed her out the door and set herself down in the basket of her beach cruiser. The bicycle ride to the Seelie Tree seemed longer than ever. This, in part, might be because she stopped for a minute at the fork in the road where the trail to Vale became visible.

Carissa looked up the mountain. The trail was empty and quiet. Far from the panic in Moss Hill, the sleepy mountain seemed still. It was to be expected. Changelings never take faerie children. But, that was precisely why they needed the help of the sidhe guard now more than ever.

"I can't go right now," Carissa said aloud.

Chaos looked up at her. She continued explaining. "It's Saturday. I haven't prepared next week's tonics. They need a few days to sit, and people depend on them. I'll go to Vale after work."

Chaos pointed at herself and then at the mountain. She looked at Carissa expectantly. Could she go on her own? Chaos was the strongest sprite Carissa knew, but if she happened upon a troll along the way, could she handle herself? She wasn't willing to risk it.

"Better stick with me today," Carissa said.

Carissa would go to see Varick, but she expected several Vale villagers to stop by as usual for their weekly herbs and health tonics. She could get a message across through them. In her mind, she was already preparing what to say to get the sidhe guard to take note without drawing the attention of the changelings as she resumed her ride around the corner of Greenfield and Gorse.

Once at the Seelie Tree Apothecary, Carissa spent a rushed morning creating her tonics at a pace enhanced by her elf-light. She'd never used magic to enhance her work like that, but she was determined to be done as soon as possible. The feeling nagged at her that she would need to close up early today.

She set up a dozen orders to be ready for pick-up the next week by the time Maren hustled through the door. She brushed off her shoulders and remarked about the state of the outdoors.

"There's a lot of snow out there today. It's piled up in the doorways."

Carissa set down the vial she was filling and walked briskly to the door. Without a word, she lowered her eyes to scrutinize the consistency of the snow. There was no doubt that there was a light flurry outside. Carissa let out her breath, visibly relieved.

"Cari? Is everything okay?"

Carissa looked up. Maren was looking at her like she had lost her mind. The initial confusion became clouded with fear the longer Carissa waited before answering. She couldn't leave Maren wondering a minute longer.

Carissa shook her head and smiled. "Yes, fine. I thought for a second—never mind."

She didn't want to explain the troll dust from the night before. That was what she'd always done, spared others the knowledge of things she didn't want to admit. Then again, the one time she'd decided to share, the night before, she ended up revealing a major secret to a changeling.

Maren seemed satisfied with her answer. She walked toward the back room, taking off her gloves and coat.

"How did your date go? Oh, wait until I put my things down. I don't want to miss a detail," she said.

Carissa waited until she returned to the counter. Then, looking right into her friend's eager eyes, she told her the harsh truth as plainly as possible.

"Cameron is a troll."

Maren's eyes widened and then her eyebrows dipped in sympathy.

"It went that badly? What did he do?"

"No, Maren. Cam is a troll, as in a changeling."

Maren paled. For the first time since they'd known each other, she seemed at a loss for words. Carissa allowed her the time to process the information by placing the completed vials on the back shelves. Chaos found the one open vial Carissa had left on the counter to lift up, ready to splash a little onto the shocked assistant. Carissa grabbed the bottle and clacked it onto the table before Chaos had a chance. She gave Chaos a glare. The faerie only shrugged.

Maren made a personal record of about a minute of her mouth opening and closing like a fish out of water. When she caught her breath again, the words flowed out. "That's terrible! How did you find out? Are you all right?"

Carissa put two hands up. "I'm fine." She filled in the details. Maren's eyes grew wider with every sentence. At the end of it, she gave a long, slow sigh.

"What are we going to do?"

Carissa smiled at the word "we." She'd had been missing out by not including Maren in the past. Cam had been the one she'd relied on before. The smile faded.

"Holly should be bringing the potions and adder stones with her this afternoon. Alden and I will hunt down the changeling imposter."

"You know, you keep forgetting something, Cari."

Carissa blinked a few times. "I do? What?"

"Me. I can help."

"I know. I'm sorry, but you have your job at Gooseberry this afternoon."

"That's no help."

"It is to me. At least one of us can have a normal day."

Maren's fingers rapped the counter.

That was a sure sign that Carissa needed to change her answer.

"We still have the necklaces to distribute," she offered.

"You were going to give those to Cam. What's the plan now?"

"I don't know," Carissa admitted. "But we've got the adder stone. We can use it to see who's human and who's just pretending to be, so we'll know whom to give them to."

"That's good, but it'll be hard to use it. I mean, we can't exactly say, 'Excuse me, could you hold still for a second while I look at you through this stone?'" Maren said.

Chaos dove into Carissa's purse, taking out the stone. Then she flew to the highest shelf of the back bookcase, pointing it downward to make her point. She held a thumbs up.

"She's trying to say—"

"Yes, I got it," Maren said. "So, we could give them out to customers today. But that doesn't take care of everyone in town."

"It does if we give them to the right people."

The right people included a few church members, a member of a school PTA, a few business people, and no one from City Hall. Not one of the people who showed up in Carissa's shop was a troll, until almost noon.

Patsy Harbridge would've been a good one to distribute the protective charms to, except that Chaos flagged her right away as a troll changeling. Carissa wouldn't have thought it by looking at her. Mrs. Harbridge had come in smoothing the strands of her updo, strutting down the center aisle as if she owned the place—in her usual manner.

She was here as co-manager of the business association; her donation clipboard gave her away. Carissa was used to bargaining with the real Mrs. Harbridge on the pledge amount until it was raised to an uncomfortable level. She didn't want to imagine how tough it would be to bargain with a troll.

"Sorry, I can't donate this month."

Rude or not, she wanted the changeling out of the store and away from her other customers as soon as possible. The troll did a better impression of Patsy Harbridge than she'd seen of the other changelings. She and Cam, could they be different types of changelings than the others had been?

"Oh, no, dear." The changeling Mrs. Harbridge lowered the clipboard. "This is a petition to separate from the Village of Vale. Businesses cannot really prosper with the people of Vale bartering or using their own ideas of payment."

"Some of them pay in gold," Carissa said.

Patsy's fake smile waned. "Not enough of them."

Her phone rang. She set the clipboard down and searched her purse, then she fiddled with the device, turning it in her hand a couple of times as the screen flipped. Her long nails tapped against the screen. She grimaced as she typed. There was a sign of a faerie if ever she saw one—most fae were technologically challenged. Finally, she managed to accept the call and held the phone against her ear.

Carissa waited. She exchanged a sly smile with Chaos, who was slapping a knee and laughing as if this troll were the funniest thing in the world. Cari stifled a laugh of her own. Chaos really needed to curb her reaction.

"Where? Who? Why would he do that? No, no, I'll be there. Yes, I'll pick him up now." Mrs. Harbridge pulled the phone away and stabbed at it until she was satisfied that she had turned it off.

"Everything okay?" Carissa asked.

"Hmm? Mm-hmm," Mrs. Harbridge said. "Timmy's causing trouble. You know how boys can be."

She did know how boys could be. Specifically, she knew Timmy and the Harbridges. Patsy would not be so quick to blame her son, and Timmy would never cause trouble unless he had no other choice.

Carissa had a horrible feeling it was something to do with the necklaces and the changeling children. When had Timmy's parents been replaced? Why hadn't he been taken? Was it the necklace, Barnaby's presence, or Timmy's own quick mind that made it so he hadn't been replaced? Whatever the case, a troll in the form of his mother was coming after him now, and she was angry. Carissa couldn't let Timmy fall into the hands of trolls.

"Maren!" Cari snuck through the aisles behind Mrs. Harbridge. Maren was working in the Otherworld today, but with her locket, she should've been able to see and hear

Carissa from either realm. She made her way to the side of the shop near the windows where she could watch the troll leave.

Maren appeared at her side by the freezers. "What is it? Why are you whispering?"

"Timmy's in trouble. I need to follow Mrs. Harbridge. Can you watch the shop until Holly gets here?"

"My gosh, is Timmy okay?"

Carissa rolled her eyes and waited for Maren to rethink her sentence.

"Oh, right, he's in trouble. Yes, go. I'll wait for Holly."

Carissa rushed out the door, kicked the stand on her bicycle up, and prepared for the elf-light to flow through her feet and speed up her journey. Chaos appeared in the beach cruiser's basket.

"It might be dangerous," Carissa warned.

Chaos faced forward and pointed ahead.

"You're the boss. Hold on tight," Carissa said.

She pedaled as fast as her feet could take her and sped down the streets, taking shortcuts where she could. She passed by the church and finally down Elderberry Road.

Unbelievably, Patsy's car pulled into the school parking area almost at the same time as Carissa turned the corner. Her blue bicycle veered in the same direction as Mrs. Harbridge only for sparks of faerie dust to catch on the tires, causing her to swerve.

"Chaos!" Carissa couldn't believe the nature faerie's recklessness. "What are you doing? Trying to make us fall?"

Chaos swiveled in the basket back and forth between Carissa and the road. She jabbed her finger wildly at the air.

"What is it?" Carissa asked. Her eyes followed in the direction where Chaos was pointing.

It was the park, the First Street Park catty-corner from the road where the school was located. Carissa rode into the park, right up to the round stones where she and her friends used to play. Where there were monoliths of open circular rocks, there were now broken half circles.

Chaos floated atop the largest one in the center before Carissa could dismount her bicycle. Once her feet were firmly on the grass, Cari stepped right up to the figures. Her fingers traced the broken stone and then came to a stop. She stayed there, processing what this meant.

"If these are destroyed, then how do we get rid of the changelings? How do we get our loved ones back?"

Chaos hovered near her. She put two consoling palms on Cari's right index finger. The half-elf stared at the nature faerie a long, long while, her mind racing in circles. She kept coming back to the same thought: without the stones, they couldn't save the children.

And she might never see Cam again.

"Of all the childish things—do you realize what you could have done?" Mrs. Harbridge's lecture could be heard across the street.

Carissa yanked her head to the side, telling Chaos it was time to go. She hopped on the bicycle and made the short trip from the park to the school lot where Mrs. Harbridge clutched Timmy's wrist and practically dragged him through the parking lot.

"Let me go! You said Barnaby could pick me up today. I'm not going anywhere with you!" Timmy wrestled against her grasp.

The fake Patsy Harbridge waved her hand in the air as if batting something away. As Carissa neared, she could tell what, or who, they were.

"Pesky faeries. Go away," Mrs. Harbridge muttered.

Hiya and Cynth circled her 1950s beehive hairstyle.

"Is everything okay here?" Carissa asked. She dismounted the bicycle.

Mrs. Harbridge stopped. She continued to hold Timmy's hand and swatted at the faeries, but she tried otherwise to maintain a civil disposition.

"Carissa, I thought you would still be at the shop."

"I asked Maren for a few minutes. It sounded like there was something wrong. I thought you might need an apothecary."

The fake Mrs. Harbridge frowned. "No one is hurt. Just a misunderstanding."

"I got rid of the changelings. Some of them. There are more, Cari, but I'll get them tomorrow."

Patsy Harbridge jerked Timmy's hand. "No, you won't. You couldn't even if you wanted to."

That sounded like a threat. She couldn't have known anything about the stones. Or could she have?

"What do you mean?" Carissa played ignorance.

A troll-like smile appeared on Mrs. Harbridge's face. "I don't mean anything except to protect my offspring."

She stormed off. Timmy's eyes pleaded with Carissa as he looked back at her. The changeling sorted through her keys and walked to her car, still gripping the boy's arm.

Her thinly veiled threat did not escape Carissa's attention and neither, apparently, did it get past the nature faeries. Before Carissa could even think of what to do next, both Hiya and Cynth blew their faerie dust in Mrs. Harbridge's direction.

The changeling swayed left, then right. Then, she fainted. Carissa could not let go of the bicycle fast enough to catch her. Chaos promptly held her arms up and strained to keep the woman in place. She scowled at Hiya and Cynth. The two got the message. They joined in, hoisting the troll up with their magic.

Now that Timmy was free, he rubbed his wrist and stared at the fake Mrs. Harbridge.

"That's not my mom, is it?"

He looked to Carissa for an answer.

"I'm afraid not," she answered.

Chaos, Hiya, and Cynth were all glaring at them now. The nature faeries couldn't keep her standing straight for long. Carissa looked around. The parking lot was empty, but

Carissa was sure it wasn't the fake Mrs. Harbridge who had destroyed the stones in First Street Park.

"We can't stay here," Cari said.

Timmy grabbed the keys. He used the clicker to open the trunk.

"We can take the car." He pointed at the bicycle.

Carissa picked up the bicycle, placed it in the trunk, and closed the lid.

"Has anyone ever told you how smart you are?"

Timmy beamed. "All the time." He held out the keys.

Carissa took them and helped the nature faeries haul Mrs. Harbridge into the back seat. She tried to make it look as natural as possible, but it would look like a kidnapping no matter what they did. Thankfully, no one was looking.

Timmy hopped in the front seat and buckled the seatbelt. Hiya, Cynth, and Chaos stayed in the back, watching over their captive. Carissa started the car, looking around to make sure no one had seen them.

"I think we're clear," Timmy said.

"I'd rather not take any chances." She navigated out of the parking lot. Mrs. Harbridge's changeling slipped onto her side. The nature faeries watched from their perch on the headrest behind Timmy.

"Where are we going?"

"That depends. Do you think it was just your mother, or is your father also…."

"They were both acting strange yesterday. I tried to tell Barnaby, but he said I imagined it."

"It was only child changelings that we knew of until yesterday," Carissa said, navigating out of the parking lot. She noticed a man in a suit jacket staring at them from a window. Another changeling? She wondered just how many there were around town.

"What happened yesterday?" Timmy asked.

"What happened today?" Carissa tossed the question back at him.

"My friends and I chased the changelings. They jumped in the circle stones."

"Adder stones," Carissa corrected, "and that was across the street."

"We looked both ways."

"Not the point. It was dangerous. What gave you the idea?" When did she start sounding so much like a parent?

Timmy's eyes looked sideways toward the nature faeries behind him.

"Was it Hiya and Cynth?" Carissa glared at the back of Timmy's seat.

"They were just trying to help."

"They could've gotten you into real trouble. These changelings are dangerous."

"All the changelings did was disappear through the stones. Until a teacher came and stopped us."

"A teacher stopped you?"

"Yes. I've never seen the teachers so mad."

"Did the teacher break the stones?"

"He was hitting them. Are they broken?"

Mrs. Harbridge stirred in the back seat. The nature faeries hit her with another spray of faerie dust, and the imposter fainted again.

"What are you going to do with her?" Timmy looked at the unconscious changeling.

"Never mind that," Carissa said. "I'm taking you somewhere safe, then we'll deal with the changeling."

# Chapter 13

## Mob Mentality and Mixed Feelings

For all Carissa knew, the police station might be crawling with trolls, so it didn't seem safe to take Timothy to the authorities. If she didn't take him to the police, Mr. Harbridge might be able to use kidnapping as a ruse to arrest her and hold Timothy captive. There were still authorities on the island she could trust—the sidhe guard.

Technically, the mayor had revoked the fae's authority in Moss Hill, even for magical crimes. Carissa reasoned, though, that her faerie blood gave her the right to seek help from Vale. Since changelings did not attack faerie people, she could bet Timmy would be safe among the people of Vale. They could also hold and interrogate the changeling Mrs. Harbridge far better than the Moss Hill authorities were equipped to do, with or without a troll presence among them.

"I thought the sidhe didn't like humans. Mayor Belkin said they were bullies."

Those weren't the exact words the mayor had used, but Timmy's elementary school interpretation was close enough.

"Mayor Belkin isn't himself."

"Like my mum?"

"Exactly like that."

She hadn't actually confirmed that fact, but at this point, it could safely be assumed. Timmy sat quietly, staring at the back seat. She hoped he wouldn't but was unsurprised when he asked the next question.

"What are they?"

Carissa glanced between him and the road. He looked like a four-year-old asking her to check under his bed for monsters. It was an easy thing to do when the monsters weren't real. How do you reassure someone about scary truths without lying? The way she always did. She told a half-truth with wholehearted conviction.

"They're faeries who can make themselves look like other people with their magic, and they got a little carried away with it. But we're going to switch them back with the right people."

"So, where are my mum and dad?"

That was the question, wasn't it? If she knew where they were, she would be rescuing them right now.

Everything is going to be—"

"Okay? Because people always say 'everything is going to okay' in books and movies right when things get worse."

"Good point. But then, how do they always end?"

"The good guys usually win."

"Then, aren't they right?"

Timmy squirmed in his chair like the seat was uncomfortable. He stared out the window. Reassurance hadn't worked, maybe distraction would. Cari switched tactics.

"When we get to Vale, I'll take you to Sal. He'll make a great, big lunch, and you can eat with the elves. How does that sound?"

Under other circumstances, visiting the faerie village might've been thrilling, but all Timmy did was shrug. Maybe seeing the fae world would help. She turned her locket and concentrated. The world around the car changed as they entered the Otherworld.

Timmy's eyes bulged, and he sat up straighter. He looked out the window in awe. The colors of the leaves, the sounds of the forest, and the car driving through it—all of it became more surreal. The world of the fae was a dreamlike realm of enchantment.

"Is this the Otherworld?" Timmy asked.

"Mm-hmm." Carissa smiled. "Listen, Timmy, I know you're scared, but…."

She abandoned the sentence. Her elf ears perked at the sound of shouting coming from a part of the forest she'd been to once before.

"What is it?" Timmy asked.

"I hear something. Hold on."

She listened. The sounds seemed to be a mess of chattering voices coming from her left, away from the faerie village. She turned the car instinctively in that direction. This brought her closer to Tabitha's house.

Timmy pointed out the front window. A group of people stood in a jumbled mess outside a white picket fence: Tabitha's white picket fence. Carissa pulled to a stop far enough away for the others not to notice their arrival.

"Take my hand," she said to Timmy. He offered her his right hand without hesitation. She uttered a short phrase in ancient druidic.

"What was that?" Timmy asked.

"It's a spell to give you faerie sight. I'm going to shift the car back to the human realm, but I want you to be able to see and hear me."

She didn't add the words "in case I need you to run." She probably should've taken him to Rolin's first, but Tabitha might be under attack this very moment. She needed to act now.

"Stay here," she said to Timmy. To Hiya and Cynth, she said, "Keep him safe and out of sight. Keep her unconscious." She pointed at Mrs. Harbridge's troll form in the back seat.

Chaos received the most crucial order of all. "Go to Vale. Get Varick and bring him here."

Chaos nodded. Carissa opened the car door, and out Chaos flew. Carissa placed two firm feet on the soil and shut the door behind her. Touching the metal, she turned her locket again. The car's coloring changed. If she hadn't used the same double sight she'd just temporarily given to Timmy, she would not have seen it at all. Leaving the vehicle, Carissa approached the people on the path ahead.

Tabitha's house was surrounded. The townsfolk had gathered into an angry mob—minus the pitchforks. Carissa pushed past the crowd, coming face to face with two uniformed officers of Moss Hill and Cameron's impersonator. Of course, the ambassador to Vale was one of the few people on the island to have a locket like Cari's. But he'd used his to shift an entire angry, frightened group to the Otherworld. The real Cam would never have done that.

"She tried to take our children, and when that didn't work, she cast her magic all over our town. Now she's made the children ill!" the impostor Cam's voice rose over the crowd.

"Arrest her!" a woman yelled.

"Come out and face us!" one man yelled.

The crowd jeered. A camera flashed. Carissa traced the source of the flash to a dark-skinned woman in a stylish grey coat holding her phone up to take pictures: Tilly Brier. She pulled the phone back, and her fingers typed furiously on the screen, then she swiped and resumed holding the lens outward. She was taking video now, Carissa realized. The reporter's sharp eyes landed on Carissa and a second later, so did her phone. Now clearly focused on Carissa, Tilly's eyes raised and the corners of her mouth pinched back so that her dark burgundy painted lips seemed to be urging her to speak up. Your turn. Say something. She was giving Carissa her chance. Cari nodded. It was nice to know there were still people in Moss Hill willing and able to hear the truth.

Cam's imposter grinned savagely while the officers trudged up to the door.

"Stop!" Carissa screeched, a bit more desperately than was dignified. "This is a witch hunt."

It was a tylwyth teg hunt, but the sentiment was the same.

"Carissa," the changeling said, surprisingly Cameron-like, "thank you for suggesting I look into this suspect." Turning to the Mossies, he said, "It was Carissa Shae who revealed to us that Tabitha was a bendith y mamau."

"Her mother was," Carissa corrected. If he wanted to play a game, she could play it, too. "She isn't one. But you are a changeling." She turned around, facing the Mossies, and pointed behind her. "This isn't Cameron Larke. There are changelings in town."

"Changelings!" a Mossie shouted. "Why should we believe that?"

"If Cari says there are, then it must be true," Mrs. Grant said, a regular customer of hers.

"Forgive me, Carissa, but if there are, how do we know you're not one of them?" Mr. Wilson said, a store owner and father to two children, a girl and a boy.

Carissa couldn't answer Mr. Wilson's question with the stone. It would not only give away her secret to finding the trolls, but could scare the townsfolk if there were other trolls among them. She had to calm the crowd, and there was only one way to do that.

"I know you, Mr. Wilson. I treated your son when he had chickenpox. And you, Jenny, I helped your daughter with her whooping cough last year. I know that you're worried about your mother's health, Morgan, and Mrs. Alcott, I know that you were nervous about a fae houseguest since you knew nothing about the Otherworld, but now you think Gilly is the best helper and friend you've ever had. I know you all well. I grew up with some of you, and I'm telling you, Tabitha is not the culprit here."

"Wasn't she a bendith y mamau? Mrs. Irving said.

"She was. You can't deny that," Mr. Smith pressed.

"That was a long time ago."

"She's put Carissa under her spell," Cameron accused. He ordered an officer. "Hold her." Fake Cam turned to her. "I'm so sorry, Cari, I really hoped you'd stay away."

The jeering started up again, but it was less enthusiastic than before. Some of the villagers were glancing nervously between Carissa and the house.

"This is fae territory," Tilly's voice rose above the crowd. Her phone turned onto Cam. "What about jurisdiction?"

Fake Cam grimaced. "The crime was against a human, so the case is ours. The mayor made himself clear about that."

"And if the fae disagree?"

"I'm the ambassador to Vale. I have that covered." Fake Cameron wasn't hearing any more arguments. He signaled for the Moss Hill police to begin. Two officers aimed a large battering ram at the door. They pounded once. Twice.

The third time the pounding was drowned out by the clomping of hooves on the forest ground. Fake Cam let out a frustrated groan and ordered the officers to cease.

"Let her go, too," he said.

Carissa rubbed her forearms and glared at the man who'd held her. He almost looked apologetic. If he really was sorry, he shouldn't have held her so tightly in the first place.

The riders halted just before the crowd. With one deft swing from his horse, Varick took to the ground and handed his reins to a subordinate sidhe guard. He strode to the gate. The humans made way for him, fully aware he was within his right to have them all arrested.

"What's going on here?" the sidhe guard asked.

Cam's impostor was prepared. He handed Varick a letter, signed by the mayor.

"We have a warrant for the arrest of the tylwyth teg, Tabitha."

Varick eyed the paper and raised a brow at Cam.

"What gives Moss Hill the right to arrest a citizen of Vale?"

"According to the charter of nineteen—" fake Cam began.

Varick wasn't interested. "That charter also gave the sidhe jurisdiction over any magical crimes on the island. Your mayor broke the charter days ago."

"Very well. We won't arrest a citizen of Vale. But we are arresting Tabitha, who lives outside of our town and your village."

The flare in Varick's eyes betrayed his rage even as he kept a calm tone. "Tabitha is fae."

"But not a citizen of Vale."

"I would like to be a citizen," a timid voice emerged behind the fence.

In their arguments, neither man nor the villagers had noticed that the door to the home had opened and the tylwyth teg had positioned herself in the frame.

Varick nodded. "She is requesting citizenship. The guard will take her into Vale. The sidhe and elves will decide if she is accepted."

"With all due respect, at this very moment, she's not a citizen."

Varick stepped closer to Cameron. The impostor flinched at the sidhe's superior height, as was, no doubt, the guard captain's intention. "A request for asylum has been made. If you have a complaint, you may bring it up with the Council of Elders."

Varick turned away. He waved a hand to one of his men, who opened the gate. Two of the sidhe guards walked past the uniformed officers and stood on either side of Tabitha. She walked out in the light-footed way of hers, practically dancing with each barefooted step. A wild thing is how she looked. Would the elders accept her as a citizen?

She almost cleared the crowd when Cameron stopped Varick with three words.

"It's for Carissa."

Varick's neck twisted back. His eyes questioned Carissa.

"This isn't Cameron," she defended herself. She should have spoken sooner. Now that the first word was his, fake Cam had the advantage. He wielded it by raising his voice above hers.

"Carissa is unwell. I think the tylwyth teg may have bewitched her. She's wreaking havoc on Moss Hill. Varick, as a friend, I'm asking you for help."

Varick stiffened. His eyes traveled between Carissa and Cam. Cari shook her head, pleading with her eyes for him to trust her.

"I have it all on tape," Tilly said.

The brazen reporter was silenced immediately by a hand signal from Varick resulting in a sidhe guard standing over her with his sword. Every Mossie knew the sidhe guard did not listen to humans. Carissa didn't blame Varick, he couldn't present evidence from a human in a sidhe court without a lot of explanation. It was "speak when spoken to" as long as the Council of Elders saw all humans as children. Carissa thanked Tilly with her eyes. Varick must have caught the gesture, but if he had, he didn't act on it.

"Very well," he said. "We will take Carissa with us. You are welcome to accompany us, Ambassador Larke. The rest of you will disperse."

He didn't need to ask the humans twice. Even Tilly apologetically walked away from Carissa. Whomever the trolls were, they gave nothing away. The changeling Cam glowered, knowing he had been foiled.

"I'm satisfied that you will handle the situation," he said.

He paused a moment as he neared Varick, whispering something in his ear. Carissa guessed it was something like "don't trust her" as one last attempt to influence the sidhe.

Then, he, too, began down the trail after the rest of the changelings. Carissa kept her eyes on him. He neared the car. She silently prayed that he did not have the double sight to see Timmy in the car. He didn't seem to. He walked right past the hood of the car and was just about to clear Timmy's door when the car suddenly shifted into the Otherworld.

Carissa's mouth dropped in horror. But Timmy flung the car door open at the same time, crashing right into the masquerading troll. Carissa ran. Varick and one of the sidhe guards followed.

Timmy stood with one foot outside the open vehicle, peering down at the troll through the window. He looked up at a breathless Carissa, grinning ear to ear. Varick and the sidhe bent over the troll, who was completely knocked out.

"It worked!" Timmy said.

He wasn't talking to Carissa. A prideful sprite made a bow from the top of the car window. The nature faeries floated to

Timmy's shoulders, each offering Timmy a thumbs up for his role in their carefully planned collision. The dynamic duo looked up at Cari for her praise. Carissa put her hands on her hips.

"I will not congratulate reckless behavior. Chaos! You could've gotten Timmy in serious trouble."

The sprite pointed at the unconscious criminal.

"Yes, I know you got him, but what about when his friends realize he's not behind them anymore?"

"Best get to Vale as soon as possible," Varick said. "Then maybe you can explain why your boyfriend was trying to arrest the caretaker of the forest."

# Chapter 14

## Forget-Me-Nots

Carissa had never drawn so many eyes to her as she walked down the paths of Vale. Curiously, it wasn't the two unconscious troll changelings on the fae horses' backs, the nature faeries sitting on the captain of the sidhe guard's shoulder, nor the presence of the human boy with two little faeries on his shoulders that caught their attention. The fae villagers stared at Tabitha. For her part, Tabitha didn't seem to hear the whispers as she went. She walked in that ballet dancing style, flowing wherever her curiosity took her until she bounced off a sidhe guard and drifted in the other direction. Since she wasn't under strict constraint, containing her was like trying to keep a bubble from floating away.

The streets were more crowded than usual, perhaps because of the mayor's ban on fae visitors in Moss Hill. The fae were grumpier for it. A few flagged down a sidhe guard to make complaints until Varick told them to move aside for official business.

Carissa was surprised when he led them not to the Redwood of the Sidhe Council nor to the Courtyard of the Elven Council, but to the home of Head Elf Rolin's daughter, Hela, and her husband, Fenigar. The naturally carved wooden house was not a place of any official business. Fenigar was a painter, a poet, a carver, and a conceptual artist, all highly valued skills among fae. But he was not a politician, and he had no authority to help Carissa in a situation like this.

"Why have you brought us here?" Carissa asked Varick as they neared the door.

"The elves and sidhe are suspicious of humans at the moment. Hurt feelings do not make one inclined to helpful actions. They are talking of full separation."

"But once they see that it's trolls—"

"Once they see that trolls have taken over Moss Hill, they will believe the unseelie have conquered the humans, and they will prepare for war or abandon the island completely. The sidhe do not believe in taking chances. Hela and Fen have made it known to the council that they do not support such actions. If we are to repair relations between our people, we must show the elders that we have a means of regaining the upper hand."

Sal opened the door. "Cari! Varick! This is a lovely surprise."

The wiry elfkin smiled so that his sharp nose looked even pointier than usual. Timmy laughed and immediately apologized, but Sal was good-natured and never interpreted an action as ill-natured.

"Surprise indeed. What are you doing here, Sal?" Carissa said as they entered.

"Yes, well, I got a little carried away with the clapping when Hela told the council they were being...ahem...I don't like to repeat it—she was brilliant defending the humans, you should've seen her. Rolin wasn't too pleased, though."

"He kicked you out?"

"Oh, he'll calm down. Everyone here is out of sorts...trying times and all. It'll blow over. Well, come in, all of you. I'll tell Hela and Fen you're here."

Varick issued an order for the rest of the sidhe to take the trolls to the prisons below the mounds. They would be interrogated later. He then entered the home behind Cari. Timmy and Tabitha both wandered in wide-eyed and awed at the size and beauty of Fen and Hela's estate. It was Fen's design, the wooden beams twisting into walls as if it had flawlessly grown into intricate carvings of its own free will. The doors and windows stretched to the sky in towering frames, and the sun played on the floor and ceiling in a prism of lights.

Varick always seemed to miss the beauty. He kept his soldierly demeanor straight up to the second-floor loft area. It was an office in that a wooden beam stood as a desk and ran to the wall where it curved into a shelf of books, lining a wall and waving up over a series of windows overlooking the outdoor garden. The shelf curved down again on the opposite wall, where it stretched into bench-like seating around a waterfall. A blank canvas stood facing everything as a final acknowledgment that the room was quite the scene to paint. Hela sat reading on the bench while Fen wrote with at his desk with a feather pen.

"That's a druidic law," Hela was saying. "It says here that in the Mossie's charter—"

"Ahem," Sal interrupted. "You have guests."

Before Sal had even finished speaking, Hela dropped the book on the seat and rushed to give Cari a hug. She even hugged Timmy and Tabitha with about three welcomes each. The high energy of the elf-woman did not put off the tylwyth teg. Tabitha hugged Hela back and drifted right over to the fountain, then to the window, admiring the vision of the fae village.

"I'm so glad you're here, Cari. I thought I'd never see you again."

There were genuine tears in Hela's eyes. Carissa smiled warmly at the overly dramatic statement. With Hela, the drama was to be expected.

"Are you studying human laws?" Carissa asked.

"We're trying to put to rest this awful business of separating from Moss Hill," Hela said.

"It won't come to that," Varick assured. "If we can find a solution to the trolls."

"There're no solutions to be found before a good meal," Sal said. "How's about helping me with baking soda bread and some mushroom soup?" Sal said to Timmy with a thoughtful nod to Tabitha.

"Do you cook with magic?" Timmy asked.

"I wouldn't know how to cook without it." Sal grinned.

"Okay. Can the nature faeries help?" Hiya and Cynth jumped at the idea of getting close to the herbs and spices in a faerie kitchen.

"Of course," Sal said.

Timmy, being smart as he was, said, "C'mon, Hiya, Cynth, Chaos, let's let go to the kitchen. The grownups have to talk."

Chaos made as if to follow. She drifted behind, watched them leave, and then zipped back to the fountain. She splashed away happily, kicking the water with her feet and hopping on the rose petals floating in it.

Carissa laughed. Timmy's always managed to surprise her with his intelligence and Chaos with her sneaky playfulness. Hela's reaction was predictable. She reached for Fen, who came and sat next to her.

"Oh, Fen, he's so adorable! When will we have one of our own?"

Fen put an arm around his wife. "All things in their own time, my love. Right now, I wonder, what is the tylwyth teg of the deep forest doing in Vale?"

Carissa tried not to see the judgment in the question. She didn't know Fen as well as Hela. She never thought of ranks or status, but did Fen share the fae sentiments of social order? Perhaps it was his ordeal with an unseelie months ago that gave him the wary eye he was looking at Tabitha with now. Or maybe it was the fact that she'd thrown toadstools at his wife recently that soured his expression.

"I was asked to come here."

Tabitha still hadn't taken a seat but had wandered to the window. She tilted her chin this way and that as she took in the view. Varick explained her presence. Carissa elaborated with the whole story of what was happening in Moss Hill.

"The poor boy," Hela said while grasping Fen's arm. "Trolls for parents. We should adopt him. Oh, unless either of you would like to," she added, looking at Carissa and giving a polite smile to Tabitha. Hela wasn't one to believe anyone didn't like her. She'd make friends with Tabitha, adopt Timmy, and start a charity for missing troll victims if no one confronted her with reality.

The tylwyth teg wouldn't be the one to do it. She didn't seem to be listening. Varick crossed his arms, tapping a finger on his bicep and shaking his head. If he wore a watch like a human, he probably would have checked it. Time was ticking away.

"We'll get his parents back," Carissa said before Hela had Timmy's entire future planned. To speed up the conversation, she added, "The problem is that we have to find them first."

"How will you do that?" Hela inquired.

"And how do we help?" Fen added.

This was where she was stumped. Varick, of course, said the trolls were unlikely to cooperate. Even with magic, they might not speak the truth. Trolls were tricky like that.

"Find the people who trust them the most. Then think of how they can use them," Tabitha said. Her arms were folded now, one of them reaching up to hold a pendant of some sort hanging from a necklace.

"What do you mean?" Carissa asked.

She turned away from the window to face Cari and the others. "Trolls get people to trust them. They'll use that trust to weave their magic. Think of how they can use the people who trust them and you'll surely find all their plans and hiding places."

"Think like a troll?" Fen shuddered at the thought.

Another thought was rising in Cari's mind. The lines on Tabitha's face deepened. She was sad.

"At your house the other day, you said not to trust Crimbal. Why?" Carissa asked.

Tabitha hid her face. Her chest hitched. The motion was recognizable to anyone who had seen it before.

"He broke your heart, didn't he?" Hela said. "I bet he did. Men are always doing that, troll, human, or any other kind." Hela grabbed her husband's arm as if she'd found the only good one and was never letting him go. As far as Cari knew, Fen was Hela's first and only love, and she'd never had any heartbreak in her life. But Hela had read human romance novels and legendary fae love stories, and so naturally she thought she knew everything on the subject.

Tabitha lowered her eyes. Carissa may have imagined it, but she thought she saw a tear drop from the tylwyth teg's eyes. From the corner of her own sight, Carissa caught Chaos pulling the handkerchief out of Fen's breast pocket. She flew it over to Tabitha, offering it to her.

"Is Hela right?" Carissa asked gently.

Tabitha looked up. Her watery eyes gave her away even before she nodded. With a slow breath, she began her story.

"When she was my mother, she was tylwyth teg, not an unseelie. Amends were given, as much as the humans wanted from her. She healed sick children, she discovered the unseelie trolls, changed some hearts, might have changed others. Not all the trolls left, you know. They loved disguises. The humans were only happy when they thought they'd driven out all the trolls. They wanted her gone, too. 'Amend' is a broken word, isn't it? It doesn't work.

"She came to the forest, where the outcasts accepted her help. The gnomes, the dryads, even the ogres loved her. She cared for them, and the fae were all right with it because the forest had a caretaker.

"From the babbling brook to the base of the mountain, my mother cared for the outcasts. Until one day, a man went to the forest and snuck out some of the magic clay to make changelings out of clay. My mother caught him, but she didn't turn him in."

"Why?" Carissa asked.

"Because a clay child is alive and it hasn't done anything wrong except being alive, isn't that right? So, she made him keep living so the maker couldn't destroy him."

"Who was the maker?" Varick asked.

She hesitated. "I don't think I know, but I knew the child. I knew all the outcast children."

So, this clay child lived in the forest? He'd have grown up by now, but Cari had never seen such a person. Had he blended in with humans or stayed outside of Moss Hill entirely? Clearly, Tabitha hadn't only befriended people of the forest, she knew outcasts who still lived in Moss Hill as well.

"One of them was Otto Crimbal, wasn't it?" Cari surmised.

Tabitha smiled, a dreamy, faraway look came into her eyes. "Crimbal and I became friends. Those were happy times." Her face was a strange green mix of tears and happiness.

"If you were friends before, what happened?"

Tabitha shrugged, turning to the window again. "I asked him not to come back, and I never saw him again."

Carissa knew for a fact that wasn't true since he'd just been at her house recently. Aside from that, there had to be more to her story. It didn't make sense. Even Hela questioned it.

"Why did you ask him not to come back?"

Tabitha couldn't speak. Carissa hated to push her, but she had to know what she wasn't saying. She tried to find a delicate way to pry further. Fortunately, Varick spoke first.

"I was not a member of the sidhe guard then, but I know the case. They suspected foul play in your mother's death."

"The sidhe ruled it a natural death," Tabitha said.

"They couldn't find any evidence, but there was changeling magic all over the room."

"It's a changeling's house," Tabitha explained.

Varick silenced himself, but his eyes were accusing. It confused Carissa. The sidhe convicted on less than circumstantial evidence. If they suspected Tabitha was guilty, why wouldn't they charge her? Was it something to do with her role as caretaker of the forest? Hela voiced another possibility.

"Did Crimbal do it?"

"He had nothing to do with it," Tabitha said, too quickly.

An awkward silence filled the room. Varick opened his mouth to say more, but Tabitha turned away again. Fen tried to smooth things over.

"Forget the past, we have to focus on finding the missing humans. Is there a place in Moss Hill where the trolls might be hiding the humans they've stolen?"

"Even if you find them, how will you stop them?" Hela asked.

"Jane is working on some potions," Carissa said. "As to the place, I have no idea."

"They use troll dust to put their victims in a deep sleep and sustain them for as long as they need. Follow the troll dust, and you'll find them."

"We already did. It's everywhere—all over town," Carissa said.

"If you can't follow the troll dust, then think like a troll," Hela suggested. "Like Tabitha said, where would a troll hide them?"

"To answer that, we must first know the troll. Who are they? Do you know which trolls have done this?" Fen asked.

"There a couple people in town I know to be trolls. I can start with them."

"I'll question the two changelings as well," Varick said.

Sal came into the room. "Lunch is served. I wasn't sure what you liked, Tabitha, so I've set out some extras."

The group followed Sal down the stairs. Varick put a hand in front of Carissa. She turned back. He dropped his arms and watched the others leave. When he was sufficiently satisfied that they were alone, except for Chaos, who wasn't going to tell his secrets anyway, he opened up.

"Have you spoken to Jane?"

"Not for a while, sorry."

"You said she was making a potion?"

"Yes, along with her brother." She hadn't mentioned Alden to the group for several reasons, mostly because the thought of an ankou was as spooky to fae as it was to humans. "It's Alden I've been speaking to."

"I see," he said, gazing at the floor as if in deep thought.

"Is everything all right?"

He hesitated. Sharing personal information was not common practice among sidhe, so pushing him wasn't going to help. Carissa waited patiently while he wrestled his thoughts.

"I sent a letter to Jane."

Carissa couldn't act surprised. Holly had told her about his relenting on the request for Jane to take an immortality elixir so that they could be together. It wasn't fair to push anyone into a decision like that. She was glad for Jane's sake that he had reconsidered.

"I hadn't heard a response," Varick said.

Carissa reached to put a hand on his arm but then hovered, not quite touching him. Such a usual comforting gesture bordered on inappropriate to sidhe tradition. The situation was strange, probably to him as much as to her.

"I'm sure she just needs time. She'll talk to you when she's ready."

"When she's ready," he repeated as if to himself. "Why, when humans have so little time, do they waste even seconds of it?"

"Varick, why are you rushing? You have a lifetime with her if she wants to be with you."

"And then eons alone," he said.

"She might still make the choice to be immortal."

"She can choose a longer lifespan. Soon, she will no longer be able to choose immortality."

"What do you mean? The sidhe won't allow it?"

He put a hand to his temple. She hated when he did that. It was a very sidhe gesture, acting as if it were painful to explain simple things to humans. He pulled his hand away. The look on his face was not condescending when he explained.

"Humans can only be immortal if they take the elixir before they begin to age. Once you stop growing and start aging, you cannot ever truly be immortal. The age is different for everyone, but she'll be twenty-five soon. It's possible it already would not work, but by then it will definitely be too late."

Now Carissa was starting to understand his pushiness. Up until now, she'd thought it was wrong for him to pressure her into any kind of decision like that. Once she realized he was fighting time itself, she could at least understand why he had been so insistent.

"Besides that," Varick continued, "she's the last of the druidesses in Moss Hill. The sidhe do not like to think of the end of things, but if she dies, there would be no more druids on the island. She will be a far easier target for the unseelie without immortality."

Carissa didn't point out that immortality hadn't helped Miss Morgan when she had been attacked by the unseelie. Instead, she said, "Jane is stronger than people think, and wiser, too. Instead of trying to protect her, Varick, you might try a far better means of helping her: trust her."

\*\*\*

ONCE OUT OF VALE, Carissa shifted back to the human realm and called her nan to make sure she was all right. Nan did not answer the home phone, which panicked her at first. At least, it did until she tried for Nan at the library and found her there. Then, it angered her.

"Nan, I thought I told you to stay home."

"And I thought it was me who told you what to do, not the other way around."

"Really, Nan, it's not safe. Mr. Greer is a—"

"He's a fine man, and I won't hear another word about it. I told you last night you need not suspect him."

"Is he there?" Carissa was losing her patience.

"Hardly anyone is here. The town is in a panic. Several more children have fallen ill. They're holding a vigil tonight at the church. I'd already told Father Quinn we would be there, unless you're saving the town."

"You told him that?"

"No, I'm asking you. Are you saving the town tonight or coming to the church?"

"Both, I think. Maren and I have more of the necklaces to distribute. I'll see if Jane is still working on the potions."

"Good. I thought we'd go around seven o'clock."

"I'll be home right before to be ready."

"You're working late?"

"Actually, I'm somewhere else at the moment, but I'll be home as soon as I can," she said as she rounded a corner and pulled into the parking lot of the Moss Hill Guardian Station.

Though the sign said Guarda Siochana, as the Irish police were generally called, here in Moss Hill the UK term "police" was more commonly used. It helped distinguish the Moss Hill authorities from the sidhe guard. And they were very different systems of law enforcement. A significant difference at the moment was the fact that some of the Moss Hill police may actually be changelings.

"Whatever you're doing, be careful, Cari."

Carissa could envision Nan's downturned lips behind the receiver. She was never one to voice her emotions, but Cari knew she worried.

"I'll be fine, Nan. See you tonight."

She clicked off the call and used her phone to take a picture of the note in her hand. Entering several numbers into the screen, she sent the photo to everyone she could think of in higher positions to get the word out across Moss Hill. She included the words: "Come to Moss Hill Guardian Station for the full story." Then, she dialed a number she never thought she'd use. The line rang as Cari opened the trunk and pulled out her bicycle. A familiar voice answered.

"Hello?"

Carissa was taking a chance, assuming Tilly was still herself, but since she'd just seen her at Tabitha's and there were enough humans with them that Cari didn't think the trolls would try anything, she bet that the reporter had not been turned into a changeling. Keeping careful awareness of how her side of the conversation would sound to anyone overhearing her, she chose her words deliberately to irk any changelings around who would be listening.

"Tilly, if you want the real story, come to the Moss Hill police station with as many reporters as you can bring with you. I've sent you a letter from the sidhe guard to the Moss Hill police stating that I've handed a child into their custody to save them from changelings—yes, that's right. No, I think Mayor Belkin's been compromised. Cam, too." She walked across the parking lot and sealed her bicycle at the racks with magic all the while continuing the conversation.

"I'm willing to bet a few of the police have been switched. Not at all, they can't arrest me. Timothy is with the changeling who is pretending to be his mother, and she was with us on the drive. I've returned the car to the police. The most they can do is question me, but it'll be hard to do with all the reporters questioning them."

Walking into the police station, she smiled as several of them stood up immediately upon seeing her. She made one final statement before saying goodbye. "If they want to check my story, all they have to do is enter Vale and talk to the sidhe themselves."

Inside, the superintendent took one look at the note from the sidhe and the car in the parking lot and let her go, though not without a grumble. At the end of her very short time there, she had discovered two things from the police station. Firstly, due to Chaos's cleverness with the adder stone, she learned that only a few of the officers were trolls. The head inspector was not one of them. In fact, Inspector Nemin seemed intelligent enough to realize some of them might be compromised. He said nothing directly, but his eyes drifted from her to Chaos, and he appeared to note which officers she was pointing out. Maybe that meant he would do something about the imposters.

Secondly, she learned from the officers' attitudes that neither the humans nor the trolls had any desire to perpetuate the story of Timmy leading a charge on the schoolyard, nor spread the knowledge that the two-hundred-year-old stones on First Street Park were broken. They were even less thrilled when Tilly and the other reporters showed up to question them about other suspected changelings in town.

They denied the changeling rumors at first, then eventually relented with a "we'll do what we can." Once it was clear that the reporters were safe and, in fact, the trolls were the ones sweating, Carissa hinted to the room that there might be changelings among them at that very moment. Carissa did not stay to see how Tilly pressed them, but if anyone could get to the truth, it would be Tilly Brier. Now that Carissa's part at the station was done, she had to get ready for the night's vigil and another confrontation with a troll she would very much like to question.

# Chapter 15

## Candlelight Confessions

People crowded around the church in masses. Father Quinn met each person at the door. Carissa did not carry the adder stone with her, and it would be too obvious for Chaos to float all over the church with it, so she left it alone. It didn't stop Chaos from throwing suspicious stares at everyone. If Father Quinn was a changeling, he was one who could undoubtedly mimic compassion well. He consoled the frightened citizens with words of wisdom and kindness so that even Carissa felt hope renewed.

"You look as if you've come to carry the weight of the church on your shoulders instead of finding solace inside," Father Quinn said as she approached.

"I'm sorry, Father," Carissa began.

"No, no. I know you have a heavy weight on your shoulders. Maren is already inside; she explained the ordeal in Vale and at the police station. I just want you to know, Cari, that no matter how heavy the weight is, you have all of us behind you, and one in particular who can help more than anyone."

"Thank you, Father. I'll bear that in mind."

"She always did carry the weight of the world on her shoulders," Carissa could hear Nan behind her. Nan carried on a conversation with Father Quinn while Carissa traveled inside. She saw Maren almost right away, huddled with a small group off to the side of the candles at the altar. Her eyes journeyed down the pews. Having found a source of interest, she took light, quick footsteps to the second row from the front.

"I know what you are," Carissa kept up her nerve as she sat beside Declan Greer.

"Do you?" He seemed disinterested. No, tired. He kept his eyes down.

In the dim hue of the candlelight, his wrinkled skin took on a ghoulish character. Now that she knew what he was, he'd never looked so troll-like.

"How many of you are there?"

"How many what?"

She set a square jaw and locked her eyes on his face. Declan Greer's head bent downward, not meeting hers. There was no way she was letting him out of this.

"You know what I mean," she said.

He held the back of the pew as if it were a crutch and leaned closer to her. Still, his eyes did not meet hers. "I don't think you know what you mean."

She began to argue, but Declan glanced at her. It was barely half a second, but the look told her enough. He was going to say more.

The old librarian sighed. "Yes, I am a troll." His faerie eyes glowed red as he finally met her gaze. "I am not unseelie."

*A likely story*, was her first thought. But then she remembered Tabitha. How many people in town were willing to attack her on the basis of her being a tylwyth teg? Carissa believed she was innocent, yet fear had almost kept the mob of Mossies from even giving her a chance to defend herself. If she condemned Mr. Greer for being a troll, she was just as guilty of letting irrational fear and bias guide her thinking.

"Do you know the trolls responsible?"

He shook his head. "I know your boyfriend was taken. I've seen the changelings, but I'm not one of them. Not all of us are responsible for this situation. We're different from each other."

"You must know them. You must know what they're planning."

"If humans started attacking the fae, would it be fair for me to ask you what they were planning?"

She bit her cheek, thinking. It wasn't the same, though, was it? Moss Hill was a human town. There were too many of them to say that everyone could be involved in a secret plot. How many trolls were in Moss Hill? It didn't matter. She had witnessed more than him just being fae.

"But I saw you talking to Cam—the fake one," she accused.

"No, you saw him talking to me," he said.

"What did he say?"

"He said if I knew what was good for myself I'd stay out of things."

Carissa bit her lip. That was plausible enough. Maybe he was telling the truth. If he wasn't unseelie, perhaps he could help act as a spy.

"You can find out what they're planning, though, can't you? They would trust you?"

"After seeing you talking to me?" He looked down the aisle at the people coming in for the vigil.

The church was filling quickly. All of Moss Hill seemed to turn out to pray for the sick children—trolls included. It ignited her faerie blood with anger. The audacity they had to attend a vigil when it was for their changeling children.... Which types of changelings were they? Was it the trolls' children for whom the prayers were made tonight, or were they the third type of changelings—the ones made of clay and magic?

"Do you know what 'crimbal' means?" Mr. Greer whispered. It was his last word before rising from the pew. Carissa stared at the librarian walking to the front of the church to light his candle. She looked at the one in her hand. Mr. Greer had intended to light the fire of suspicion, but would trusting him blow up in flames?

\*\*\*

"YOU SEE?" NAN SAID as they drove home from the vigil.
"I told you it wasn't Declan Greer. I've known the man all his
life. Even if he is a changeling, a troll, or whatever, I know
people. He's not a bad one."

"I admit, he doesn't seem to be disingenuous," Carissa
agreed.

"Never argue with the driver"—is what Nan always used to
say. She had to admit, he didn't look guilty. But if she'd
learned anything over the last few days, it was that looks could
be deceiving.

Right now, Otto Crimbal, who was shaking hands with
Father Quinn, looked the picture of kindness.

"Nan, stop the car," Carissa said. She opened the door at
the same time, jumping out before the vehicle could stop.

"Cari! You could at least wait until—"

The door slammed shut.

Carissa pulled her coat tighter around her and walked
briskly in a drizzle of rain. Crimbal turned away from Father
Quinn and began walking into the church. He didn't hear
Carissa call his name simultaneous with a crack of thunder.

The second time, he stopped at the door and turned an
ear. She tried his first name. "Otto. Do you have a minute?"

The fae man turned around. His black coat flared lightly
from the wind. Despite the cold, he followed Carissa outside.

"Miss Shae, I'd ask you what this is about, but given the
circumstances...." He looked back at the church.

She asked him point blank: "What does the word 'crimbal'
mean?"

"Crimbal?"

"Your last name. It has some meaning."

"I know my own name, Miss Shae."

His icy stare made the air seem colder. He was like a frozen statue. It made it seem all the more incredulous when he broke his gaze. When he spoke, it was like she'd lit a fire under him.

"A crimbal is not a troll child—it's not alive at all."

"The clay changeling," Carissa recognized the type from Alden's explanation and Tabitha's story.

She looked at him with wide eyes. A question inevitably rose beneath her eyebrows. She pinched her lips together so she wouldn't ask. It didn't matter. He knew what she was thinking.

"And now you think I'm not real?" Otto Crimbal stood tall with defensive eyes.

Tabitha never spoke clearly, but she would have said it if he were the clay child from her story, wouldn't she? The crimbal in her story grew up in the forest, Carissa was almost sure of it. She shook her head.

"No, I'm sure you're a troll's child. But you have the name, why?" she had to ask, but she apologized with her tone.

Mr. Crimbal sighed. His old, wrinkled hand touched his forehead.

"It was a cruel joke—to give me the name."

"Who gave it to you? The family who took you in?"

Crimbal nodded. "Dr. Torreng. He took me in, gave me a home and a family, but I could not share the last name. He wanted me to remember that I was a changeling and not one of his own."

There was such sorrow in his voice that Carissa almost felt for him. Tabitha's words still pulsed through her ears.

"But Tabitha's mother was willing to give you a home."

"Not a home: false friendship. She turned me out of the house and away from her and...."

"And Tabitha's mother? Did you kill her for that?"

Mr. Crimbal's eyes widened. "No, of course not." His face paled. "Is that what Tabitha thinks?"

"She has reason enough to believe it. It was troll dust found around their home. She didn't want you to be blamed, so she covered the evidence and said nothing. If she hadn't been a bendith y mamau, the sidhe would have given the investigation more scrutiny, but you got away."

"No, not me. I would never have done that." He closed his eyes. "If she would've talked to me."

A tear rolled down his cheek. Surprised by the emotion, Carissa placed a hand on his arm.

Crimbal opened his eyes.

"Do you think that she...."

Carissa knew what he was asking—whether Tabitha would believe him. She was stubborn and still angry. Would she listen? She had let him into the house a day ago, but this afternoon, it seemed that Crimbal had broken Tabitha's heart. But was he innocent? Or only pretending to be? She was inclined to believe the former, but not confident enough to try to convince Tabitha of it.

"I'm sorry," Carissa said.

He sniffed, straightening. He tried to cover the emotion. "No, I suppose not. It's all water under the bridge. Doesn't matter now."

"But the children do. It's important, Mr. Crimbal. We know there are changelings in town. Do you think these ill children are crimbals?"

He shook his head. "I don't know. Maybe."

"If they are, how can they be switched back with the real children?"

"No single spell undoes them. There are stones—"

"The stones on First Street are broken."

"Then only powerful magic can unmake them."

"What kind of magic?" Carissa asked.

"Changeling magic is binding magic. You'd have to find the person who switched them before...."

"Before the changelings die?"

Crimbal looked away from her as if struggling against tears. Carissa understood that she'd brought up old memories and emotions. Still, she had the sense that he was holding something back.

"If you know anything else—"

She'd sparked a flame with those words. A surge of anger flooded from him.

"All I know is that unseelie trolls are greedy. They don't leave their children because they want what's best for them. They do it because it's best for them, the parents. More riches, more influence, more power, whatever position the child could take that would place the family in power. And there's the irony. Because trolls are both loyal to their own and uncaring at the same time. But there are a few, some seelie trolls, who do care for their own children and the humans around them. They'd never give their own away and maybe take in others, too. And if a troll should be born in such a family, they are luckier than I."

At the end of his passionate speech, he swiveled on his heels and strode into the church without another word. He was bitter, enraged at what life had given him, and all Carissa could think was poor Mr. Crimbal. It must've been hard living among humans without the company of his own kind. But then, there was Mr. Greer, passing him on the way out. Briefly, his gaze looked back and forth between Carissa and Crimbal. His eyes widened into a question.

She smiled and shook her head. No, she didn't suspect Mr. Crimbal. Satisfied, he nodded and walked away.

"I told you it's not Greer," Nan's voice made her jump.

Carissa put a hand over her hear, catching her breath as she answered. "I don't think it's him either."

"Then why did you jump out of the car like a crazed cat?"

"I had another theory."

"Oh? So, who was it?"

"No one, never mind. Let's go home," she said.

It wasn't Mr. Crimbal, and it wasn't Mr. Greer.

# Chapter 16

## Break-Ins and Broken Hearts

The rain let up, but the wind was unrelenting. The car turned around the corner at the top of Crescent Circle to the sight of a man clamping a hat down on his head as he wrestled his keyset and walked down the Cartwright's driveway. His vehicle, a clay-red sedan, was not one Carissa recognized. However, she did catch a glimpse of his face as they drove past.

He was familiar, but Cari couldn't quite place him. She couldn't resist the urge to talk with the stranger. Carissa wasn't ignoring anything at the moment. Besides that, she had to check on James's findings from the hotel.

Nan pulled the car into their garage. She was either a mind reader or knew Carissa's puzzled expressions well enough to tell the difference between them now.

"I'll leave the garage open, close it when you come in," Nan said.

Carissa nodded and opened the door in a snap. Chaos was soon at her shoulder, though she was yawning and flying like a sleep-dazed sprite. Carissa turned around to see Nan walking inside. The nature faeries sat half-snoozing on her shoulders. Carissa held a palm flat for Chaos to land on.

"You did a lot today, Chaos. I'll be all right. I think I know who it is, and I just want to talk to him for a minute."

Chaos rubbed her eyes and gave a lazy salute, then drifted off inside the house. Carissa crossed the street to where the man was already opening his car door. She called out before she reached his vehicle.

"Dr. Torreng?"

The man turned around. Now that she could see his face, she was almost certain it was him. She knew all the doctors and nurses on the island, if only on paper. She was reasonably sure she'd seen him in passing.

"Yes?"

"How is the Cartwright baby?" She assumed that was why he was here.

"She's well," the doctor responded.

Carissa was relieved to hear it but skeptic at the same time.

"Her parents called you?"

He shifted on his feet. "I thought I'd check given the state of the other children on the island."

His words were caring, but the tone was matter-of-fact. And there was the little matter of it being eleven o'clock. Carissa asked, "They were all right with you visiting so late?"

"I think they were just happy to have a doctor make sure she's okay."

"Of course," she said. A thought occurred to her. He was the personal physician of Mayor Belkin, so maybe he could help with the whole situation of the mayor being a changeling.

"Dr. Torreng, have you seen the mayor recently?"

An eyebrow twitched, and he tilted his head curiously. She almost felt she'd struck a nerve. Maybe he had already suspected that the mayor was not himself.

"He had his physical just days ago. Why?"

"Did anything seem off about him? Was there anything unusual in his behavior or his test results?"

"That is privileged information, Ms. Shae. I wonder why you're asking it."

"You know about the changelings in town," she argued. "It's a reasonable question to ask since—"

"It's a rude question to ask, and I won't answer it. You are not the mayor's pharmacist, and as a medical professional, I expect you to know better. Now, I'll forget you asked it and be on my way."

She was taken aback by his rough tone. Inwardly, alarm bells were ringing. Was he merely a doctor trying to protect a patient's privacy, or was he covering for the mayor's impostor? Could he really have treated a troll changeling and a crimbal without noticing either one was not human? Rather than make an outright accusation, she made an apology, smiled as kindly as she could, and headed toward the Cartwright's front door.

Once he was behind her, she dug into her purse to find the adder stone. Where had Chaos put it? There, her fingers touched the edge. She retrieved it and turned, hearing his car engine start at the same time. She lifted the stone to her eye too late; Dr. Torreng was already driving away.

She did, however, see Anne opening the front door. At least Anne was human. Her neighbor looked confused and maybe a little tense.

"Is he gone?" she asked.

"Yes," Carissa answered. "Why? Did he try to hurt you?"

"Hurt me? No, nothing like that." She relaxed. "Oh, it's probably my imagination. I'm always like that when James works a night shift. I heard about the changelings. Then the doctor rushes in here to see Alayna. She's fine. He was perfectly fine, too," she said quickly. "I don't mean to seem ungrateful. It was nice of him to check on her, I just thought...but he did act a little odd, didn't he?"

She seemed to be asking herself the question. It only confirmed Carissa's suspicion that he might be a changeling, too. If he were, the only way to sort that out would be to find the trolls responsible.

"Don't worry, Anne. We're trying to find out. I'm glad Alayna's okay. James mentioned something the other day about the visitors at the Failte Abhaile."

She shook her head. "I knew it. He mentioned it a little when they first arrived. He knows I worry about him snooping around. He could lose his job or," her eyes widened, "could he be putting himself in danger?"

"No, I'm sure he's all right," Carissa said.

She didn't know that to be a fact, but Anne obviously needed reassurance. Although she probably wasn't wholly convinced, Anne took a breath and seemed to calm herself. Carissa tried a softer approach this time.

"When does he get off work?"

"He'll be back around midnight and then up again to go in at 7:00 a.m. They have him working such long hours lately." Anne pushed a hand through her frazzled hair.

Carissa pulled her lips to the side in a sympathetic smile. Anne was the picture of a tired mother.

"Will you tell him to call me when he gets in or at least before he leaves tomorrow? I won't ask him to do any more digging, but maybe something he's found out so far will help catch the people responsible for the changelings."

"Are they really all over town?"

"I think you'll find a few of them exposed in tomorrow's news."

"That's something then. If my James can help with that, I'm glad. Just promise me you'll keep safe, and keep him out of trouble, too."

"I will, I promise," Carissa said.

She almost immediately regretted it. How could she promise to keep anyone safe? She'd do her best, of course, but could she really be sure she'd succeed in doing so? She wasn't even sure she'd be able to save Cam.

Anne Cartwright closed the door and before Carissa could turn around, there was Chaos, practically smacking into her forehead. The nature faerie frantically signed and pointed back at the house.

"What is it?" Carissa asked.

From the way Chaos was pointing, she expected to see her house on fire. Everything seemed fine. Still, the nature faerie yanked Carissa's elfish ears and rammed her back.

"Okay, okay, I'm going." She hurried across the street and into the garage, closing it behind her. It wobbled a little as it went down and there was a gash in the door leading into the kitchen. Why didn't she notice these things before? Inside was a mess—and not just the kind the nature faeries made whenever they decided to raid the cabinets for sweets.

"What on earth?" Carissa muttered while rounding the kitchen island.

The fridge had spewed its contents on the kitchen counter and floors. Spice and herbs spilled from open cabinets. Hiya and Cynth cried over the remains of a honey cake smushed on the floor as if they were in mourning.

Carissa walked toward Nan's room. The dresser drawers had shifted from their usual positions, and the clothes had tried to make a run for it. That, or they had been robbed.

Chaos tugged Carissa through the hallway to the sitting room. Books lay sprawled across the floor. Cari picked up Nan's poetry book, *Tea and Roses*, that had landed on a couch cushion by the fireplace. She'd have set it on the bookcase if it were still upright. She placed it on the coffee table instead, then moved on.

The upstairs was no better. Glass cracked beneath Carissa's shoes. The wall was bare, and the picture frames lay on the floor. Carissa imagined her own room was likewise in disarray. She would've checked, but once she reached the landing, her eyes were immediately drawn to Nan, who stood outside the study.

Cari shut her eyes and hoped beyond belief that the room was untouched. She knew that would've been the intruder's purpose. But how could anyone get in? She and Chaos had put spells all over the house, doubly so for the study. Carissa moved forward.

"It's still locked," Nan said as she approached.

But Nan kept staring at the door. Cari's grandmother was not the type of woman to show fear, but she was pale as a ghost, and her eyes darted up and down the door as if she could not believe what she was seeing. Bracing herself, Carissa turned her eyes to the door.

Deep gashes cut into the thick, sturdy wood. The wounds on the door were covered in the same white powder as much of the town: troll dust. It shimmered like snow on a sunny day.

Carissa tried the knob. Some dust fell. A sheen traveled down the door in a wave as if a wobbly bubble over the entrance refused to pop. The magical barrier was still in place, and the door was still locked. Carissa and Chaos looked at each other. Without a word, both put up their hands, palms facing the room, and concentrated.

The bubble traveled down and dissipated at their feet. Carissa turned the knob again; this time it opened. Inside the room, all was well. The books sat in their proper places on the shelves. The desk stood sturdy as a sentry overlooking the room. There was a mess in one corner of the room, where Maren had left a pile of books that Cari had not had the energy to clean up. Carissa picked up the stack, chuckling.

"I'm glad you find a robbery amusing," Nan chided.

"The magic held. I had no idea what I was doing, and it held. Maybe it's the old magic in the room. Whatever it was, we're fine. Nothing magical was taken. No one was hurt."

She stopped rambling, realizing both Nan and Chaos were looking back and forth between her and each other. Nan put her hands on her hips and stared at Cari as intently as she'd studied the door.

"You're taking this much better than I expected," Nan said.

"I am," Cari said. Then, she paused. She was, wasn't she? Why was she taking it so well? Her shoulders raised as she crossed her arms and wandered to the desk. "I guess I'm relieved about the room, but it's more than that. For the first time, I read about magic, and I could use it, really use it, to hold up a powerful spell. That troll must have tried hard to get into this room, and my magic held."

"You're part Tuatha de Danann, Cari. Training or none, you shouldn't be surprised that your magic is powerful. Only, I wonder why anyone was able to break into the house at all."

"Chaos and I put magic on the front and back doors. We didn't think to protect the garage door. It was a mistake. We can do better next time."

Carissa rested her fingers on the desk. She thought about her grandfather sitting in this very same room, writing his knowledge for posterity, reading the older books from previous druids and fae. What would he have taught her if he'd lived?

"I hope there isn't a next time, Carissa. These trolls seem determined to steal your grandfather's secrets," Nan said.

Carissa took one more look at the room before walking out of it. As she helped Nan clean the mess the robbers had made, she thought about the prospect of any unseelie getting their hands on the magical knowledge and treasures the room contained. She hadn't yet learned a fraction of the secrets her grandfather had stored in that study. How much damage could the unseelie do with knowledge like that? She was determined not to find out.

*** 

MAREN DID NOT take it well over the phone the next morning. Carissa almost regretted calling her, but she and Nan hadn't finished reorganizing last night, and she knew if she didn't show up to church, Maren would conjure up all kinds of reasons why she wasn't there. All would be catastrophes, of course, and Maren would be a wreck imagining each one. She wasn't much better with the news of the break-in.

"Oh my goodness! Are you okay? You could've been killed!"

"We weren't home. We were at the vigil, remember?"

"Yes, I remember you only talked to me a few seconds between cornering your suspects. How did that go?"

"I don't think it's either of them. But I started reading more of my grandfather's books, and I may have something to help defeat the trolls."

The truth was, she'd abandoned the cleaning after about an hour and then spent most of the night in the study. She couldn't help it. It was too much knowledge to ignore.

"What did you find?"

"Trolls don't just steal people. They steal magic, too, which is probably why they were trying to break into the study."

"That's logical."

"Funny you should use that word. Logical is one thing trolls are not. From what I was reading, they're highly emotional. They are some of the most reckless fae, which means they'll just as easily go after magic they have no chance of getting as magic that's easy to get regardless of consequences—if it's a big enough prize."

"So, whose magic is a big prize in Moss Hill?"

Carissa bit her lip. Her own magical heritage was still secret in Moss Hill, but was it secret to the unseelie? They'd already come after her grandfather's study, which made sense if they knew her grandfather was a descendant of Queen Maeve, a Tuatha de Danaan. Was her family's power the biggest prize in Moss Hill?

"What I don't understand," Maren said without seeming to care that Cari hadn't answered, "is if they go after riches and powerful magic, why are they going after children?"

"To get to the parents, I'd think."

"But why the Cartwright's baby? They aren't rich or powerful."

That was a good point.

"Because James works at the hotel? He mentioned some of the guests being odd. Maybe the trolls just had access to him."

"But they didn't make him a changeling. Why his daughter?"

Again, Carissa could see her point. Why would they use a baby? She thought back on events over the last week. The first people to act strangely in town had been the children. The Cartwrights were among the first of them to be affected. Affect the children first to get to the parents? But they were more selective when it came to the adults.

"Maybe it was random?" Cari suggested.

"Like practice? They just used whomever they had access to?"

"Well, if the visitors at the Failte Abhaile are involved, that would explain how they could have targeted the Cartwrights. I'm not sure how they got to other children."

"You're assuming the people at the hotel were working alone," Maren said.

"Good point," Cari replied.

Maren was full of good points today. Maybe Declan Greer was innocent, but that didn't mean the rest of the Greers were as guilt-free. If they were trolls, perhaps they weren't the seelie fae they pretended to be.

"Thanks to Tilly's blog and the Mossie Insider News, everyone's pressuring the mayor's office to find the culprits. But, I think I've found them myself." Carissa could picture Maren beaming with pride. It came through in her tone, which humbled itself the next second.

"Well, no, it wasn't me exactly. Reginald sent me another letter. He said Mrs. O'Mally is, get this—"

"A troll?" Carissa asked.

"Yes. How did you know?"

"Mr. Hart hinted at it, but it's not surprising given what's going on."

"Maybe you'll be surprised by this: she was bragging to Reg and the prince that she had family coming to Moss Hill."

"At the hotel? I just talked with James Cartwright this morning about a family we suspect might be involved with the changelings. He's meeting me there in a half hour."

"Be careful, Cari. If she was bragging about it, maybe it's because they're too powerful to fight off easily."

"I don't plan to fight them at all. I'm just meeting with James, and Chaos is going to look through the adder stone to see which people are trolls and which ones aren't. I'll be in and out quickly."

Maren was quiet for a minute. Carissa nearly asked her what was wrong. Sounding as if she'd been debating whether or not to say something, she finally spoke.

"Cari, there's something else, it might be nothing, but...."

"But what?"

"I saw Alden at Gooseberry yesterday in the Otherworld. I forgot to turn the locket back so I could still see into the Otherworld…well, that doesn't matter. Anyway, Alden was meeting with Varick."

"So?"

"So! You said the sidhe don't like ankous."

Carissa bit her lip. There was so much she hadn't told Maren. It had slipped her mind entirely to tell her that Varick and Alden had worked together before. But once she revealed that they were acquaintances, Maren should've been able to see why they would have something to speak about.

"Maren, you know who Alden is, don't you?"

"Of course I do. He's Alden Everly. He was a friend of Cam's who studied abroad, some kid who went to high school with us. Just because I didn't recognize him doesn't mean I wasn't listening when Cam explained."

"Who else do you know named Everly?" Carissa challenged.

Carissa waited for the realization to sink in. Two seconds of silence was followed by a gasp.

"Jane! Of course. Varick is in love with Jane, and he's Jane's brother!" Maren shrieked.

Carissa winced. Maren never took the sensitivity of Carissa's elf ears into account. She wasn't done.

"You think Varick was talking to Alden about Jane? Do you think he's trying to win her back?"

For all her talk about writing off men, Maren certainly took an interest in other people's love affairs.

"I don't know. And you shouldn't jump to conclusions," she chided.

"Are you going to ask?"

"Ask Varick about his love life? No. Anyway, I did talk to him yesterday. I was probably the one who gave him the idea to talk to Alden."

"How did you do that? What did he say?"

"Maren, it's not my place to tell."

"He told you something secret!" Maren exclaimed. When she was met with silence, she mumbled something about how Cari always kept secrets from her.

"He hasn't heard from Jane, that's all. He wrote a letter, and she hadn't replied. Happy?"

"But why is she avoiding him? I saw them at the Christmas party. It really looked like they were in love. I need details."

Carissa rolled her eyes. They had been fighting at the Christmas party in Vale. Later, Alden had been at Carissa's house on Christmas Day, and Maren had utterly missed the fact that he was Jane's brother. She didn't have an excellent record for noticing details.

"Maren, it's none of our business."

"You're no fun. Ugh, if only I hadn't seen their secret meeting, then I wouldn't have to wonder."

Carissa's hand shot out, smacking her own forehead. "That's it!" She was the one shouting this time.

Maren's perplexed voice raised. "What's it?"

"You wouldn't have seen it if you weren't looking in the Otherworld!"

Silence came from Maren's end of the receiver. Carissa explained.

"Don't you see? Things in the Otherworld are hidden from humans. Only fae folk can see them. What is the one thing the mayor asked for from the people of Vale before people around Moss Hill started acting out of character?"

"He asked the sidhe guard to stay out of Moss Hill—oh! I see! The changelings are hiding people in the Otherworld."

"Right under our noses. They could be in their own homes. The troll dust could be keeping them frozen, like a magical time-freeze."

"So, they're in their own homes sleeping? That doesn't make sense. Holly could see into the Otherworld at the Cartwright's; the baby wasn't there. And Barnaby lives with the Harbridges, so I'm sure he would have noticed if they were unconscious somewhere in the home. He literally occupies the same space in the Otherworld."

Carissa bit her lip. Maren had an excellent point there. So, they weren't in the homes, but the people had to be somewhere in town. What was a place in Moss Hill where they could store frozen humans without people noticing them?

"The hotel!" Carissa exclaimed. "They're keeping them at the Failte Abhaile."

"It could be. But the place is swarming with trolls. How're you going to get in?"

"I already have someone working on that." She thought of Mr. Cartwright. It was time to check in on the manager-turned-spy.

# Chapter 17

## Finding the One

Carissa had set the meeting place as the back entrance to the Failte Abhaile. The time was 7:00 a.m. She tried to discreetly slip into the kitchen unnoticed. She'd even worn white to better blend in with the chefs. Her auburn hair was pinned tightly into a bun, except for that one stray lock that kept falling out of place. She tucked that behind her ear, where Chaos was hovering.

"Okay, you know the plan. You'll hover up near the ceiling and check out anyone inside through the adder stone."

Chaos gave an eager nod. The adder stone rested firmly in her hands. With her back to the wall, Carissa counted to three in her mind. Then she opened the door, took a step inside, and pinned herself to the wall by the light switch. Unfortunately, this accidentally switched the lights off. Rather than turn it back on, she froze.

There were no outraged voices, no one asked who had turned off the lights. The windows offered a dim view of the room, just enough to see by. Cautiously, Cari turned her head. There was no one by the stove or the counter spaces. She shifted her eyes to the right.

The light flicked on. A hand caught Carissa's arm, and she gasped.

"It's all right." The hand let go. "It's me."

She turned right toward the door to the dining hall to see James Cartwright holding two palms in front of him. Carissa put a hand on her heart.

"You scared me half to death."

"Sorry, I had to make sure it was you. I didn't want anyone to know I was meeting you here."

"I hope you don't mind. We have to make sure you're you," Carissa said as she looked up at Chaos, who gave her a nod. James was human.

He nodded. "I understand."

"Have you found anything?" Carissa asked, relieved that he was himself. She really had expected this to be a trap. Now that she knew it wasn't, she hoped it would lead to answers.

"A lot. There's evidence of something odd all over the place. That's why I asked to meet here. There's the kitchen menu—all root vegetables and tree bark on the menu. There's a white powder over everything."

Cari shook her head. All of that was fitting with trolls. The diet of the root vegetables especially rang a bell. She remembered seeing Mrs. O'Brien and Mr. Burrows both buying root vegetables at the Seelie Tree. Maybe this hadn't started with just the kids. Maybe they were replacing anyone they thought could give them an advantage. Mr. Burrows and the Harbridges had their business contacts, Mrs. Obrien was the wealthiest Mossie, but why switch out Alayna? To get her father to trick Carissa into meeting him here?

James continued, "The oddest part is in the rooms. More and more of the rooms are being left with a 'Do Not Disturb' sign or with special instructions to the cleaning staff not to go into the restrooms. It's like they're hiding something."

"What about names? Is there anyone named Farthing staying here?"

"Yes. There are four groups from what I can tell. Some are the Greers' cousins. Some are Farthings. There are a few—"

The door opened.

There was Mr. Greer, the hotel owner, with a raised eyebrow and a scowl on his face. He crossed his arms. In a gruff voice, a question boomed from his lips.

"Cartwright, why is there a non-staff member in the kitchen?"

Carissa stepped forward. "Sir, I'm—"

"I know who you are."

Carissa bit her tongue, briefly glancing at Chaos. There was a shocked expression on the nature faerie's face. What did that mean? Was Owen Greer a troll or not? Had James led her into a trap?

The owner dabbed a handkerchief on his reddening face. There was a moment of awkward silence as Carissa recalled his son's misdeeds and her own uncovering of his role in certain crimes. He likely was thinking of it, too. Even if he was human, and an innocent one at that, she could understand why he might still hate her. It wasn't a surprise when he pointed a finger to the door.

It was not the back door, though, but the dining hall door he'd just come through where he directed her to exit. She and James complied. The hair on the back of her neck rose as she wondered whether this was the trap.

Owen Greer asked as they walked, "What are you doing here?"

His bitter tone made the question sound more to Cari like she wasn't welcome here.

"Sir," James tried to explain as they walked, "I asked her to come, I was concerned—"

"I was asking her. And what exactly do you mean, you were concerned?"

James opened his mouth, but the owner interrupted again.

"Never mind. I want an answer from you, Miss Shae."

Out in the lobby, the television was on. Carissa could hear it in the background.

"*...It was revealed last night that changelings may have infiltrated—*"

"I'm sure you've heard the news," Carissa said. "It must be concerning to your guests."

He was a good actor, joining his wife at the concierge desk with a puzzled expression. Arda Greer gave Cari the same look of surprise as her husband.

"Why would the changeling news concern our guests?" she asked.

"Maybe because they are trolls," Carissa replied.

She looked triumphantly up at Chaos. The nature faerie shook her head. Cari's mouth dropped open. The Greers weren't trolls? The hotel owner crossed his arms again. Carissa wasn't sure what to do. She looked at Chaos again. The nature faerie pointed in two other directions. First, she singled out a man talking on a cell phone by the elevator. Next, there was a woman in the lobby sitting on a sofa in front of the giant television screen. She took her eyes off of the screen and was looking intently at Cari and the Greers. Carissa reached a hand up, taking the adder stone from Chaos. The sprite would need her hands free if it came to a fight.

"I'm not sure what you and your sprite are trying to do, Ms. Shae, but I will call the police, whether they're humans or trolls, to have you removed from my property."

Carissa glanced at the woman. She was still watching them, but she was also sitting for the moment.

"Just one question," Carissa said. "James, could you please explain to Mr. and Mrs. Greer about your suspicions?"

The Greers turned to him. James began nervously shifting his eyes to his feet and between the two of them. He rambled quickly through his list of observations.

Carissa took the opportunity to wave Chaos over to the computer. The nature faerie, she'd learned months ago, could not only read but loved technology. If she could press the print button on the keyboard, Carissa might be able to swipe a copy of the guest list.

The woman across the lobby rose and began walking toward them. She must've seen what Carissa was doing. Mr. Greer had also heard enough from James.

"None of what you said constitutes proof of any foul play. I suggest you refrain from making wild accusations or you will be excused from your service here. As to you, Ms. Shae, unless you have real evidence, I advise you to stay away from the Failte Abhaile and my guests."

Cari looked at the woman approaching them and then to Owen Greer. "Here's my evidence: I can prove here and now that you have a troll resident in your hotel. I think the sidhe guard and the Moss Hill authorities will both be interested in the troll visitors who showed up precisely when changelings began taking over the town."

"A horrible stereotype," Mrs. Greer dismissed. Her fingers gripped the counter, and her chest rose defensively.

"It's bad enough you exaggerated my son's…mistakes, but now you're accusing me of what, exactly?"

"I think it's obvious," said the woman who was a troll. "She is accusing you of being responsible for the changelings. And based on what I've seen, I wouldn't be the least bit surprised if she was right."

The woman's tone was warm, and nothing about her seemed troll-like. Without the stone's magic, she had the appearance of a pleasant, aging woman with white-blonde hair. She extended a hand to Carissa.

"Perla Greer."

Carissa was not fooled. She responded with a warning.

"I've already informed the sidhe guard of my suspicions of the hotel. If you're thinking of any violence against me, they'll know exactly who to investigate," Carissa said.

She didn't also tell them that Alden was just outside waiting for Chaos to pop out to get him at any time. Let that be a surprise to them. She had come prepared.

Mrs. Greer slapped the counter and pointed to Perla. "That's exactly why she has to hide. She is a seelie troll, but Mossies will never stop being prejudiced against trolls of any kind."

Perla put her hand up. "It's all right. The town has just been threatened with changelings. It's understandable. Ms.

Shae isn't evil for thinking it's us. My grandson, Declan, has always spoken highly of her and her grandmother."

Carissa looked at the floor and then back up again. Part of her felt this was a ruse, but another part recognized that there was truth in there, too. There was a feeling rising deep in her chest and stinging at her eyes. Shame.

"I-I'm sorry." She blinked.

"Get out," Mr. Greer said.

Perla waved a hand, gesturing for Carissa to walk with her toward the front entrance. "Owen, don't be rude. Ms. Shae, would you speak with me a moment?"

Carissa followed Perla to a sitting area near the main entrance.

Perla continued, "There are things I think most people don't know about trolls. For one, most of us are seelie now. We live among humans. We've scattered all over the world, blending in. We can live apart for many years, but then we long to see other trolls again. That's why we have reunions, like this one. We chose Moss Hill because of the people. We heard Mossies were the friendliest."

"You heard it from Declan or, forgive me, but, did you try to?" Carissa asked.

Perla smiled the way Nan used to do when Carissa was completely missing the point of a lesson. "I do speak with my grandson, Declan, often. He speaks highly of you and your grandmother. He apparently hasn't opened up to you about his past, though.

"The last time we lived in Moss Hill, there was one family who was very kind to us. Their son and ours became friends. When a family discovered that one of their children had been replaced with a changeling, all the trolls were banished. But my grandson, Declan, so loved the Greers and Moss Hill, he begged to stay. The Greers agreed to take him in."

"You didn't take the Greer child and replace him with Declan?"

Perla laughed. "Who told you that? No, no, the Greer child you speak of is Owen's father. They grew up like brothers."

"But you left, you just abandoned your grandchild to the Greers?"

"To family. The fae don't generally take last names, but we trolls do because we blend in with the humans. It's our way of life. My family and I took the name Greer. We had to leave Moss Hill for a time, but we've always thought of this island as home."

"That's why you want it back."

Perla sighed and took a seat in one of the chairs by the door. Cautiously, Carissa sat next to her. No matter how bad she felt for accusing Perla outright, she had to remember there were a lot of missing people in Moss Hill right now, and the visiting trolls were the most likely suspects.

"Ms. Shae, four families are visiting Moss Hill right now. Of the four of us, there are two who used to be unseelie."

"The O'Mallys are one," Carissa accused. "One of them has already been caught in…somewhere else." Cari did not want to give anything more away like she'd done with her grandfather's study. She had no desire to cause any trouble for Reg on the island of the sidhe and elves.

"Which other family was unseelie?" she asked.

Perla shook her head. "You're wrong. The O'Mallys are not unseelie. As to the others, I won't just assume they are guilty. If you insist on searching, you should also know that when the trolls were asked to leave, not all did as they were told. It may not be anyone here who is involved. Now, I'll do what I can to help the sidhe and the Moss Hill authorities, but I won't betray innocent trolls. I hope you won't assume we're all guilty."

Carissa softened a little. Perla seemed genuine in her statements.

"I don't want to blame innocent people either," Carissa said, "but you could at least give me the names of the unseelie families."

"I think you'll find a list of all the families in the report you swiped from the printer with the help of your nature faerie." Perla stood up. "I want to believe that you'll be fair and that the sidhe will not just assume guilt, but I can't just take your word as I know you won't just take mine. I'll give you exactly which family is involved when I discover who is involved. Until then, please excuse me."

Carissa watched her walk away. As she passed the concierge desk, Owen Greer's eyes rested on her and then traveled to the door and back to her again. She understood the message: Now will you leave?

Carissa had no choice but to respect the hotel owner's request. She got up and walked through the revolving door. Outside, Chaos called to Alden in a wave Carissa couldn't quite follow. Her summoning brought Alden in human form to their side. His disguise of a black hooded jacket and sunglasses weren't entirely transformative, but at least his skin was not see-through.

"Are you all right?" he asked.

"Yes," Carissa said as they walked around the side of the building to an alleyway.

"How did it go in there?"

Carissa pulled the guest list out of her purse. "I managed to get this."

She unrolled it and held it between them. She and Chaos looked at each other, recognizing one of the names immediately. Alden gave a blank stare.

"What is it? Do you recognize anyone?" he asked.

"I think I just found the culprit," Carissa responded.

"That's great! Should we take it to Vale?"

Carissa shook her head. "Take us to Jane. Then get everyone: Varick, Maren, even the head inspector. I think it's time we chase these changelings out of Moss Hill."

# Chapter 18

## Love and War

The Everly estate was a sight even in melting snow. The mansion was a mix of stone and wood, with towering turrets and raven statues on either side of sweeping steps leading up to an impressive set of dark-wood double doors. Alden brought them right to the entrance and rang the bell.

The home of the druidess was protected with layers of spells. Carissa did not know whether this included her brother's ankou powers or if he was just being courteous by not startling Fudge, the butler, with a surprise appearance. Fudge's generally stoic expression almost turned to a smile upon seeing Alden at the door. It soured as Alden explained the situation. Carissa was sure he could not have been happy with the prospect of a house full of guests while the heads of the household, Jane's parents, were away on business.

The tall, silvery-haired elfkin showed Carissa and Chaos through the house while they awaited Jane's arrival from church. Carissa noted the changes in the home since Jane's apprenticeship as a druidess. The halls and doorways were enchanted. Carissa could feel the magic like a slight pressure in the air as she passed through each entrance. The main hallway led to the living room.

"Miss Jane was able to create the potions you and Holly needed," Fudge said.

He brought them right to the walk-in pantry. It seemed like an odd place to store magical items. The contents were mostly standard: sugar, flour, canned goods, pickled vegetables. Fudge turned what looked like a support pillar for the shelves, and the entire shelving pulled back. A whole new set of shelves were revealed in the secret compartment. It startled Carissa and made her wonder: Did everyone in Moss Hill have a room of magical secrets?

Chaos clapped her hands and flew over everything, reading every label. She threw a bit of faerie dust on one, just to see the reaction, a flash of color. She also caught Fudge's sleeve. The dapper gentleman flicked the dust away, eyeing the sprite with a frown. She gave a sheepish grin and floated over to Carissa. Reaching for a few vials at the center of the shelving, Fudge handed two slim, pink and one thick, yellow bottle to Carissa.

"To transform the changelings back to their original form," he said for the pink ones. With the yellow, he hesitated and leaned forward. He spoke in a low, stern voice. "To take a changeling's magic. This is not to be used lightly; a few drops will steal the magic temporarily. Use the whole of it on one changeling, and all of their magic will be gone forever."

She held the two vials in one hand between her fingers. The large one cradled in her right palm held her attention.

"Don't drop it," Fudge ordered. He pulled the pillar again and gestured for her to exit first. Carissa stepped away from the transforming pantry.

Fudge rummaged through a drawer or something. She could hear the scraping sound of sliding compartments. When he emerged, he brought with him a handful of adder stones.

"To see the changelings," he said.

Cari looked at the stones. They were just like the one Chaos had been using. Ancient magic is what Alden had said. Cari marveled at the craftsmanship. This was what Jane could do in just a couple of days?

Fudge set the stones down on the counter. At the same moment, she heard a confused voice somewhere in the house.

A series of questions shot off, one after another. It sounded like the head inspector of the Moss Hill Guard Station.

"Wha-what are you? Where am I? We were just at the station. How did we get here?"

Carissa set the jars down on the kitchen counter and followed Fudge into the living room. She found Inspector Nemin gripping the fireplace mantle. Alden turned to Carissa with a shrug.

"I tried explaining—a little," he said.

"Not enough," Fudge said.

Carissa waved to Alden. "Go. I'll handle this."

His disappearing only left the inspector more shaken.

"I demand to know what is going on here."

"Inspector Nemin, I believe I have the answer to the changeling problem."

"Only fitting, since you blew it all up yesterday."

She held her anger. Chaos didn't do as well. The sprite had one hand on her hip, one pinched in the air like a mouth. She open and closed it mocking his words. Carissa put a hand around her waist and gently pulled her face to face. She shook her head. Chaos scowled, but she stopped.

"Please, have a seat, inspector," Carissa insisted.

"If I'm not needed, I shall see to lunch," Fudge said.

The butler bowed and exited the room. Carissa walked to the sofa. Chaos followed, sitting on the back of the couch. The inspector warily took the chair opposite them.

"There was a rule in Moss Hill, years ago, that all trolls must leave the island."

"All unseelie trolls. I know of the law," he said.

"You're right," Carissa said. She had read it in her grandfather's journals. "But there was already a law that all unseelie fae must leave. Why a separate law for the trolls?"

"I think it's obvious. It's all this business of changelings."

"Yes, but, such a law singling out one kind of fae, I would think it would cause the trolls to interpret the law as I said it before: all trolls must leave the island."

"You think they've returned to seek retribution?"

"They wouldn't be seelie trolls if they did. No. But I do think some stayed."

"You're talking about the crimbal."

"Mr. Crimbal is one, there are others. As a troll recently told me herself: trolls blend in with humans. I think there are some who have been pretending to be human for a very long time."

"You're saying there have been changelings here for a hundred years?"

"Not changelings. I don't think they stole people, not at first. I think they just blended in."

"Trolls do blend in very well indeed. What have I missed?" Holly's sudden appearance caused the inspector to jump.

Alden, who'd brought her, already made his exit. The bean tighe sat beside Carissa. She held two hands out over the table, looking around.

"Fudge? Is there no tea?" Holly called out as daintily as a person could shout across the room.

A grunting sound came from the kitchen.

"Thank you!" Holly replied. "Now, did you find the potions?"

"Yes, Holly. Fudge already gave them to me."

He had given them to her, but they were technically sitting out in the kitchen. Holly seemed to notice, but rather than saying anything to her, she pulled out the mushroom mix from her large bag. She popped the cork.

"Excellent." She held up the vial as if ready to throw it on a certain frightened human. "Are we sure he's not a troll?"

It was a good point. Carissa looked at Chaos. She rolled her eyes and drifted to the kitchen, where Carissa had set down her purse.

"Chaos will check," Carissa said.

She was trying to be prepared, but she was new to this role. She hadn't exactly volunteered to be the protector of Moss Hill. It was difficult to think of everything.

"I am not a troll." Inspector Nemin looked very much offended. "But I would very much like to know why I've been brought—"

"You fool!" a booming voice interrupted the inspector.

Varick and Alden appeared beside the sofa. The fair-skinned sidhe sported a bruised cheek. The sight of it pushed Carissa to her feet.

"What's happened?"

"Your boyfriend got away," Varick waved a hand. "Don't argue, I mean the fake one. Now, where has the ankou gone?"

Varick made a full circle and pounded a fist on the couch. Alden had disappeared again. The sidhe let out a frustrated groan. "That impertinent druid!"

As if he'd heard, Alden reappeared. He gripped the back of the sofa and shook his head.

"I've lost him," Alden said.

"You should've let me handle him."

"He was about to attack you with changeling magic."

"I am a sidhe. Changeling magic is nothing to me."

"Then how did he get away?"

"Boys!" Holly's voice was loud enough to startle everyone. Once she had their attention, she said in a drastically softer tone, "We're about to find out if the inspector is a troll."

Varick's hand immediately flew to the hilt of his sword. Every eye raised to the nature faerie hovering above Inspector Nemin's head. Chaos, ever the drama queen, savored the attention. She slowly lifted the adder stone to her face. Lowering it with exaggerated pace, she shook her head.

Sighs of relief went all around, except for the inspector, who demanded again to know what was going on.

"A group of trolls just checked in a few days ago for a convention, but there were others here on the island already…."

Carissa caught the inspector up on what the rest of them knew so far. She included the letter from Reg and her discussion with Mr. Hart about Mrs. O'Mally. Holly chimed in a time or two until Fudge brought in the tea and she asked about lunch. Or, actually, she instructed him about lunch, finally deciding that he needed help in the kitchen.

Maren and Jane arrived just as her mention of Mrs. O'Mally was ending. She and Jane, both in their Sunday best, were a sharp contrast to Carissa's slacks. Jane was a vision, to Varick more than anyone. Cari could see the stars in his eyes. Jane blushed and pushed back a strand of her dark hair. Carissa also caught the way Alden's eyebrows twisted. It wasn't exactly disapproval, but more a reminder that Jane was the ankou's sister.

"You will never guess what we found out at the church." Maren poured herself a cup of tea and helped herself to the sandwiches Holly was bringing out.

Jane pinched one delicately between her thumb and two fingers. Inspector Nemin had either relaxed or was just too hungry to scowl anymore. He took one with a "thank you" to Holly. Fudge glowered at the stolen credit and disappeared back into the kitchen.

Maren continued, "Mrs. O'Mally is not whom we think she is. Guess what her maiden name is."

"Torreng," Carissa said.

Maren stopped, holding her sandwich just short of her open mouth. She lowered the bread and straightened. "How did you know?"

Carissa unfolded hotel paper on the table and pointed. "The name was on the guest list. Plus, Dr. Torreng was on my street last night when my home was broken into."

"I would bet he was the one who did it," Maren said.

"Right," Cari said. "According to my grandfather, the trolls have a head of the family, generally the one with the strongest magic, because they can bind the rest of the family with their power."

"That's why changeling magic is so strong," Holly confirmed.

"If it's Dr. Torreng, then finding him would make the others less powerful," Alden explained.

"If the sidhe were allowed into the city, you would not need to weaken the others. We could arrest them now," Varick said.

"Belkin just ordered a complete separation this morning. Any fae citizens of Moss Hill are to be escorted to Vale. He's making a speech at the square, probably right now. The order goes into effect tonight."

"That's not fair!" Maren said.

"That's the point, dear. He's giving the trolls an unfair advantage."

"What about half-fae?" Carissa asked.

"I-I'm not sure," the inspector replied.

"It doesn't matter. He's not Mayor Belkin. He's a changeling. All we have to do is expose him. Mossies won't listen to him after that. Once we get the real Mayor Belkin back, it'll all be over," Alden said.

"I'm not sure about that," Varick countered.

"What do you mean?" Cari asked.

Varick looked at her, at all of them, as if it should have been obvious. "You see this as his first attempt at separation from the fae, but that's not true."

"He's right," Alden said. "He is the one who pushed for the restoration projects, increasing tourism, even advertising to put Moss Hill into public awareness."

"He had permission from MacLir. Cameron knows him, and I know Cam, he would've seen it if Belkin was a troll."

"That's what trolls do, dear. They win trust and loyalty, they charm you," Holly reminded.

"It was Belkin who came to my father with the idea of Everly Exports. He was the one who asked us to contact MacLir."

Carissa couldn't believe it. Could Belkin be a troll? Until today, she would never have entertained such a thought. But then, Perla had said something she didn't need to admit.

"One of the trolls I spoke to said that there were two unseelie troll families in Moss Hill. The Torrengs are one, what if the Belkins are the other?"

"It all fits," the inspector said.

Everyone looked at him. They waited for him to elaborate. He looked at them in surprise.

"Well, I thought everyone knew. Belkin's older brother was engaged to a Torreng, a girl named Tamsin, but then they called it off. They're close as anything the Torrengs and the Belkins."

"Tamsin," Carissa sat on the edge of her seat. "Mr. Hart said that was Mrs. O'Mally's first name."

"So, she's the one who was making trouble in Tir-Na-Nog. They had this whole thing planned," Holly said.

"So, what do we do?" Maren asked.

"You will expose the mayor to the people of Moss Hill, and I will detain Dr. Torreng," Varick said to Inspector Nemin.

"You'd better let me come with you," Alden said.

Carissa made a suggestion, "Or better yet, you and the inspector gather your men and find the Mossies being kept at the hotel. Your officers can use the adder stones to see the trolls. Alden, Jane, and I will find Dr. Torreng, and Holly and Maren can expose the mayor."

Varick may have frowned, but he recognized the reasoning behind the plan.

"Very well," he said.

He stood. So did Alden, but Varick put a hand up.

"There are other ways to travel. I'll see myself out." He shared a brief glance with Jane and then disappeared to the Otherworld. Carissa could still see him with her double sight, and quite possibly so could Jane, whose eyes followed him out of the room.

"I'd rather see myself out, too, if you don't mind. I'll have the officers meet me at the hotel," the inspector said, taking out his cell phone.

"Well, I, for one, would rather travel with an ankou. Never thought I'd hear myself say that." Holly chuckled. "Come, take us to the square, my dear."

Alden glanced at Carissa and Jane, saying, "I'll be right back."

Jane sat silently, smiling sympathetically at Carissa. "Alden told me about Cameron. That must've been difficult, to see someone you love as a changeling."

"It was, but we'll get him back, I know it."

Jane nodded. Her eyes drifted to the floor. Carissa had only known Jane a short time, and in that time, she'd only seen Jane grieving. First at the loss of her brother, then losing her dear fae friend and teacher, Miss Morgan, then at the upset with Varick. Now she seemed to be flittering between emotions. Carissa didn't feel right prying, but she had to ask.

"Jane, how have you been?"

It wasn't just a passing pleasantry, but a genuine asking of the question.

"Fine," her voice wavered.

Carissa stared at her. Jane lowered her gaze, but Carissa did not relent. Jane sighed, giving in to her stare.

"I've told Varick that I cannot be with him."

This was not a complete shock. Jane and Varick's relationship had been on and off for at least the last few months. Cari didn't want to interfere with what seemed like an unstable romance, but Jane seemed to want to talk about it. And, in all honesty, Carissa was curious.

"Can I ask why?"

She shrugged. "Alden suggested I take some time for myself to see what I really want."

Carissa agreed with Alden. Jane was young. Varick was young for a sidhe, too, she supposed. He had asked too much of Jane too soon, but he was learning. Varick had all the arrogance of a sidhe, but he'd also changed a lot in the short amount of time Cari had known him. Perhaps one day they would return to each other, but for now, it was wise to step away.

"You deserve happiness, Jane. If you need time to find it, give yourself that time. If you and Varick are meant to be, then you will end up together, and no force on earth will stand between you."

Jane smiled. "I know the same is true for you and Cam."

Alden reappeared. "Are we ready?"

Carissa stood. She was ready to get Cam back. Nothing would stand in her way.

# Chapter 19

## Bonds of Friendship

Dr. Torreng was not in his office. Alden took them every place they imagined he could have gone. His home, her own home, the hospital, City Hall—he was not in any of them. They even tried Crimbal's home and office, both of which were empty.

"Could he be at the hotel?" Jane asked.

"Can't you sense him?" Carissa asked.

Alden shook his head. "I can only sense danger, places where a soul is about to be taken."

Carissa sighed. "We'll get nowhere like this. We might as well try the hotel. If he's not there, we can at least help the police and sidhe arrest the others."

"Perhaps we'll discover something once we're there," Jane suggested.

Alden agreed. He placed a hand on both of their shoulders and shifted again across Moss Hill. Carissa was starting to feel sick from the journey. This time, however, the nausea was overbearing. They ended up outside on their hands and knees. Carissa put a hand to her forehead to stop the dizziness.

"What happened?" she asked.

"Magic," Alden groaned. "The building is shielded with it."

A sidhe guard came to her aid. She noticed two others doing the same for Jane and Alden. Once the world stopped spinning, she saw it was Varick at Jane's side.

"We're trying to get in, but it's too strong of a force."

"What have you tried?" Jane asked.

She stepped in front of what seemed like an army of officers, taking the lead. Testing the barrier, she put a hand out and touched the building. A shifting hue of colors radiated over the magical barrier.

"I can take it down. I just need a little time," Jane said.

"If we found Torreng, this could go a lot faster," Alden said to Carissa.

"You haven't found him?" Varick seemed to be reprimanding them.

Carissa wanted to argue, but now wasn't the time. Where was Dr. Torreng hiding? Or was he hiding at all? She recalled how angry Crimbal had been at discovering that Tabitha thought he was responsible for her mother's death. What if Torreng had killed her? When Cam went after Tabitha, Carissa assumed it was to use her as a scapegoat. What if there was more to it than that?

Trolls loved power. Did Tabitha's position as guardian of the forest give her a power Torreng wanted for himself? She did watch over the clay from which the crimbals could be made. If he wished for unrestrained access to the forest, he might have gone to try for Tabitha again.

"I think I know where he is," Carissa said.

The wind picked up, and thunder cracked overhead. Jane's spell over the building caused a glow over the whole structure. The force of it was powerful enough to affect the weather. The trolls inside were looking angry on the other side of the window. Some held their hands against the glass, as if strengthening the barrier.

Alden joined his sister. His ankou magic doubled their power. Unfortunately, this caused an uproar of chatter from all the spectators. Some Mossies would surely recognize him out in the open like this. Alden was revealing himself to all of

Moss Hill. But, the trolls' resolve was breaking as they realized they had no chance against them. Even little Chaos's hands on the building seemed to be doing something.

"They will stay, let's go." Varick yelled. He called for one of his horses and grabbed Cari's hand. They rode against time. Hopefully, they could catch Dr. Torreng and stop Crimbal from becoming unseelie himself.

* * *

CRIMBAL LOOKED LIKE a 1920s American mobster. In a long coat and fedora, all charcoal black, he held a pistol in his hand. He had his victim cornered.

Dr. Torreng's wide eyes followed Carissa and Varick from the trees to the brook where they were standing. He said nothing, just stood there, hands up and sweating in the cold. Crimbal didn't acknowledge their presence, though he must have seen their shadows as the evening sun stretched them down the hillside.

"Crimbal? What are you doing?" Carissa held two hands out, palms facing the ground.

What that was supposed to do she wasn't sure, but at least it showed she had no elf-light charged and wasn't carrying a weapon. In contrast, Varick's hand gripped the hilt of his sword.

"How did you find us?" Crimbal asked.

"Tabitha. We thought Torreng might've gone to her."

"He didn't make it."

"I know. I knew you'd try to protect her. And I knew you'd come here. You didn't know you were a crimbal, did you? When I told you about Tabitha's mother, that's when you realized the truth."

"And you knew I'd bring him here?"

"I guessed. It's the only place on the island where the clay exists that made you."

The gun shook in Crimbal's hand. His skin took on a reddish hue, matching that of the rocks and soil around them. His voice cracked as tears rolled down his cheeks.

"He took everything from me. Now they're taking from all of you. I won't let them destroy Moss Hill."

"So you're going to, what? Take down all of the trolls from the convention, one by one?" Carissa asked.

"I only have to take down this one." His pistol dipped to indicate the doctor.

"I'll handle him," Varick said.

"No." Crimbal's response was sharp. "He's mine." Crimbal's eyes remained locked on Dr. Torreng.

"Killing him won't help us," Carissa said.

"It will only cause you further isolation from the town you love." Varick's attempt at persuasion impressed Carissa. It was quite possibly the first compassionate handling of a potential criminal she'd ever seen from a sidhe guard.

"We need him," Carissa said. "It was you who said that the troll who created the magic can undo the spells binding the changelings with the humans they've stolen."

"Any powerful magic can undo the spell," Crimbal said.

Carissa shook her head. "It will be easier with his. And you won't be a killer."

She ventured a step forward. Crimbal cocked the gun.

"You don't know what he took from me."

Carissa stepped back, palms straight up now as if she were a hostage. In her calmest voice, she said, "I do. I know that you loved Tabitha."

Crimbal shook the gun, still pointing it at Torreng.

"He lied to me. He told me that it was the Declan's family who abandoned me, that they didn't want Declan or me. I thought we were the same, both abandoned. But each time the trolls visited the island, they accepted Declan as their own. He had two families. But me? They didn't even know me. Do you know how much that hurt? It made me turn away from Declan. Then, Tabitha, she turned away from me. I've been alone." He looked at Torreng intently. "And it's all because of you, isn't it? You formed me from the clay, then Tabitha's mother discovered your creation. She kept me alive, and you killed her for it, didn't you? You made Tabitha hate me."

Dr. Torreng did not speak. If anything, he clamped his mouth shut tighter.

"I want to hear the truth from your own lips. Answer me!"

The troll's silence broke. "You are an abomination! You're not even a troll, you're a thing! If that tylwyth teg hadn't cursed you to be alive, we'd have dissolved you before the humans had even found out! You're no Torreng. You are nothing but a crimbal!" He spit out the words with venom.

Crimbal paled a shade more with every word, each one a slap in his face. His breathing became erratic. His voice became menacingly low.

"Whatever I am, it is because you made me."

His fingers barely moved before Varick acted.

"Enough of this," the sidhe said while simultaneously lunging forward with his hands charged in magical energy. He sprawled a hand flat across Crimbal's back, and a jolt surged through the man.

Torreng took this as his chance to flee.

Without thinking, Carissa leaped after him. The troll was fast. Hurling over boulders, ducking under branches, and zig-zagging through the forest, he ran. Carissa's pace just barely kept with his. She wasn't gaining any advantage.

Overhead, thunder cracked, and a light drizzle of rain intensified. Carissa blinked as the raindrops fell faster. Torreng blurred and dipped in and out of sight as he ran too quickly through the uneven terrain.

He was quick, but she was a half-elf. What a troll could manage in speed, she could outmatch in endurance. They had the whole forest to put their wills to the test. Torreng was only traveling deeper into faerie territory.

And deeper in were the homes of the unwanted fae. Some Cari had never met, but others knew her well enough to want to foil the troll's escape.

Carissa became aware of the eyes watching them first. A face or two popped out of the trees. The red-hatted duegars, the shy gnomes, a dryad or two, all gave them their attention. A quarter mile in, a group of duegars joined Carissa.

"Need help?"

"We could push him in a hole."

"Or keep chasing him, the ocean cliff's not far away."

The group's suggestions continued. Their piping voices caught the Torreng's attention. He glanced behind him with a wicked smile. Then, he sped up.

"I'm fine!" Carissa said. "I don't need help, thanks!" She, too, tried increasing her speed.

It turned out there was no need. Torreng's braggadocious turn caused him to trip. He tumbled to the muddy ground with an "ugh." When he scrambled to his feet, the old troll was not alone. Noz, the big-nosed and big-hearted bugul-noz, rose with him.

"Sorry," Noz said slowly, not yet understanding the threat Dr. Torreng posed. "I wasn't expecting—"

"Don't come any closer!" Torreng yelled.

He grabbed Noz by the nape of his neck. Cari stopped. Her heart was already pumping, though, and that meant the elf-light gathered naturally at her hands. She kept her palms in fists at her side. There was no need to tip him off. The rain was letting up, and Carissa could see them more clearly now. Torreng had a firm hold on his captive.

"Turn around and walk away, or this faerie dies."

"Dies?" Poor Noz's already exaggerated features widened in shock.

The duegars grumbled. One pumped his fist. Another bent forward as if preparing to run.

"Don't!" Carissa put an arm out to signal the duegars to stop.

Torreng took it as an attack. He held Noz up by the neck, pulling him back and upward. The troll dust frosted around his neck. The helpless, hairy fae man began to choke.

The duegar made for a crash course with the troll. Torreng was too quick for him. He thrust Noz toward the duegar, hitting his target right at center. Though he turned with just as much speed, Carissa lashed out before he could run again. The effect was not as intended. Instead of a jolt of elf-light, it was a smoky wind that rushed like a cloud over Torreng. It knocked him from his feet.

She knew it shouldn't have been her first thought, but either Carissa had imagined it, or the smoke had been a rosy pink. Maren—it had to be her fault. She was always getting into her head like that. Would Cari be stuck now with pink Tuatha de Danaan magic for the rest of her life? Was that a good thing or bad? She wasn't sure.

But she did have to snap of it. Standing there staring at her hands wasn't helping. Dr. Torreng scrambled to his feet and began to run again. Carissa rushed to Noz.

"Are you all right?" she asked.

He sat up with the duegar's help. "I'll be fine."

Carissa turned her attention to the receding form of the troll. She stood and readied herself to continue the chase. "Good, stay here," she said.

This time, with her new magic still swirling around her, she tried attacking as they ran. She aimed her hands at Torreng's chest. The mist shot out like lightning, but it was all smoke. Now she was running through a pink fog in which it was difficult to see.

"Great," she muttered.

With a little concentration, the fog dissipated. Carissa tried again. This time when she aimed, something like bubbles formed in the air. One caught Torreng's foot just by luck. He flipped and spun in the air, landing squarely on his face.

She came within inches of him, but he was already rising to his feet.

"You're no elf." He gripped his chest. "What are you?"

Carissa didn't respond. If he didn't know, she had no intention of telling him. He wasn't interested in an answer anyway. Still sitting where he'd fallen, Torreng held his palms steadily, hovering above the ground. A low rumbling began at her feet. Carissa looked down.

They'd come to an area without grass, where the rain had turned the ground to mud. Forms started to rise up, surrounding her in a circle. She gasped as the realization of what was happening sank in: Torreng was creating crimbals.

Carissa turned in a circle, watching the ground form faces, shoulders, and torsos. She raised her hands, but the pink mist became wispy puffs of air. Then, as if the wind blew them away, she lost her powers completely.

She could hear her heart thumping as her fear grew. She still had her elf-light. She closed her eyes and let the feeling of her old familiar magic fill her veins. Before the magic found its way to her hands, Cari heard a squishing sound. It was the sound of clay smushing down on itself. Cari opened her eyes to see the forms flattening back in the earth.

Torreng's eyes widened. For the first time, she saw in them genuine terror.

Carissa turned around. The green form of a tylwyth teg lowered her still-glowing, green hands. It was clear she was the one whose magic had dissipated the mud-forms. That alone was impressive, but more so was that fact that Tabitha was not alone.

The gnomes, duegars, dryads, wood nymphs, and many other forest fae stood with her. Torreng tried to run, only to find an ogre at his back.

"Are you all right?" Tabitha asked Cari.

"Thanks to you," Carissa said.

"And thanks to you, I know who really killed my mother."

Tabitha ignored Torreng. Instead, she walked next to Carissa and waited with her for the sidhe to arrive. Within a minute, Varick made his way through the forest to take the trapped troll into custody. He'd brought two sidhe with him. Crimbal walked behind them, timidly glancing at Tabitha. Carissa nudged the tylwyth teg toward him.

Cari and Varick watched the happy couple reuniting for the first time in so long. Carissa crossed her arms and gave a sigh of relief. Then, she remembered what Crimbal had almost done.

"What happens to Crimbal now?" she asked Varick.

Cari worried the elders might punish him for his actions, or worse—they might call for his return to clay. She had understood Crimbal's anger, but the sidhe almost certainly would not.

"I did not see him pull the trigger. Did you?" Varick asked.

Carissa nodded. If he wasn't going to tell the sidhe elders, neither would she. Crimbal might have a chance at a new beginning after all.

# Chapter 20

## Romance and Rescues

Carissa entered the Failte Abhaile before Varick, having run inside the moment they arrived in front of the building. The hotel was now packed with cuffed trolls. Grumbling complaints had filled the lobby. Some of the Moss Hill police argued back, others silently led the criminals to the police cars. The Greers stood behind the concierge desk, arguing with Holly.

"You cannot do a room search without a warrant. This isn't fae territory, and the mayor declared—" Mr. Greer's jaw fell mid-sentence as Maren turned up the television. A hush fell over the lobby as a woman standing in the center of the town square reported the news.

"*...Earlier today when Mossie Maren Raines and her fae assistant, Holly, threw a potion on him. It's unclear at this point whether the mayor is a changeling or has been a troll all along. Unverified sources suggest the latter is true. Either way, one thing is certain, the mayor has been taken into police custody and will be under investigation.*"

"Fae assistant?" Holly shrieked. She grabbed the controller from Maren's hand and muted the story. "And what do they mean 'unverified sources?' I told them that myself!"

Gasps and whispers traveled through the room as the rotating doors spun open. Maren finally noticed Carissa was there and walked toward her. She had to wait a moment and let a half-dozen sidhe guards drag in their chained captives. The sight of Dr. Torreng stunned the captured trolls into silence.

"He's already undone the binding. Check the rooms," Varick ordered. The sidhe dispersed.

Maren appeared at Carissa's side.

"Where's Cameron?" Cari asked her.

"We haven't found him yet. The Harbridges are fine, though."

"This was your doing?" Mr. Greer stomped toward them. He was stopped by two officers. "I should've known."

"You should've known that a group of trolls were using your hotel to steal humans," Maren said.

"That's ridiculous," Mr. Greer retorted. "We've seen no evidence of that."

"This is discrimination," Mrs. Greer added, falling in line behind her husband.

"No, it's not." Perla Greer stepped away from a group of police officers and headed over to the door. She brought James Cartwright with her.

"Did you fire this man?" Perla asked.

"He was fired the minute the police attacked my hotel," Mr. Greer replied sharply.

"You won't have any repercussions against Mr. Cartwright," Perla said. "He was brave enough to seek out help when he saw trouble. He ought to be rewarded for it."

"It's people like him who—"

Perla held a hand up. "He and Ms. Shae discovered a near takeover of Moss Hill." She smiled at Carissa. "And she was honorable enough to find the real culprits instead of attacking all the trolls."

"We know it wasn't all of them, Mr. Greer," James explained.

Carissa helped him out. "It was the Torreng family, using the convention as a cover. We're not sure if all the Belkins were involved, but anyone following Dr. Torreng's orders will be prosecuted according to sidhe law. No other trolls will be held for anything that's happened here."

Mr. Greer shifted his feet. Mrs. Greer's eyes scanned the room as if trying to confirm the statement.

Cari stepped toward them, and the officers parted to let her pass. The Greers' eyes shifted away from Carissa as she approached.

"Could you show us all the rooms the Torrengs were in?" she asked them.

Perla gave them a piercing look. Mr. Greer relented. He and his wife led them over to the concierge desk.

"Here." Mr. Greer set a map on the counter. He looked between the blueprint and the computer screen, marking x's as he went.

"Which one would Cameron be in?" Maren asked.

A fluttering of faerie dust covered the desk. Carissa and the others looked up. Chaos flew above Carissa's shoulder, pulling her by the ear.

"Ouch. Okay, I got it. I'll follow you," Carissa said.

"Wait," Maren said, "how do you know we got them all? Should you take a sidhe guard with you?"

Carissa looked around for Varick. There he was, by the elevators with Jane. His hand cupped her cheek, and she nodded. She was all right. Satisfied that she was unhurt, the sidhe walked back to his guards.

"I'll go with you. My people caused this mess. The least I can do is help the humans get out of it," Perla said.

Maren pulled Carissa aside. "You should get Alden or Varick to go with you."

"There are sidhe everywhere," Carissa said, "and Perla has only been helpful so far. I'm going to trust her."

"I hope you're right," Maren said.

* * *

THE FAILTE ABHAILE Hotel took on an unnatural pallor in the Otherworld. The lights flickered over the grey and white imperial trellis carpeting. Movement behind Cari cast shadows on the floor.

Carissa turned to see a sidhe leading a captured troll through a perpendicular hallway behind her. In front of her, Chaos led the way. She seemed to sense something. Perla agreed with the sprite.

"This was the hallway where the Torrengs were staying," Perla said.

"Any idea which one Cam would be in?" Carissa asked.

They moved forward. A door opened. A sidhe guard blinked upon seeing them, then apparently decided they were not a threat and went into the next room. Edwin Burrows exited the room behind the guard. He clutched his head.

"Ugh." The dazed Mossie rubbed his temples and looked up. "Carissa? What's going on?"

"It's all right, Mr. Burrows. You're safe."

"Where am I?" He looked around.

"The Faitle Abhaile," Perla told him.

"How did I get here?"

"There are officers downstairs to help you. They'll explain everything."

Mr. Burrows nodded and wandered past them. Sidhe guards and human police using adder stones walked in and out of the rooms. Confused Mossies staggered out after them. Perla in her human form helped direct them to the elevators. One officer tried to keep her away, but a sidhe explained that the Greers were trusted in Moss Hill.

Carissa opened the doors. She was looking for Cameron, but she couldn't ignore any other Mossies in the hotel.

She helped a few more, all the while growing more nervous about Cameron. She found Mrs. O'Brien slumped in a chair in one of the rooms. None of the sidhe must have entered this room to wake her yet. The white troll powder covered her, but more than that, it had frozen her like fossil covered in frost. She was cold to the touch.

Carissa had no clue how to undo the spell. She tried to use her Tuatha de Danann power. How had she done it before?

She looked at her hand. She tried envisioning the swirling pinkish-red cloud around her hand. Nothing happened. She tried using her emotions. She placed her hand on Mrs. O'Brien's shoulder and drew on her desire to help her. The elf-light rippled through her heart. It was magic, but the wrong kind.

"How do I do this?" she asked Chaos.

The nature faerie frowned. She put a hand to her chin and squinted her eyes as if in deep thought. Carissa put her hands on her hips and stared at the sleeping Mossie. A sidhe guard entered the room. Seeing that she was there—and perhaps assuming she had it under control—he turned back.

"Wait," Carissa said.

The guard's ears twitched. He looked at her. Cari pointed to Mrs. O'Brien, asking, "How do I wake her?"

The guard stomped toward them. He stopped beside Mrs. O'Brien's chair and held a hand out. His blue sidhe light engulfed his hand like a flame. Touching her forehead, he closed his eyes and the flame grew to envelop Mrs. O'Brien's face. Her eyes fluttered open.

"Oh my," the waking Mossie said. "What's happened?"

"Everything is fine, Mrs. O'Brien. There's a woman in the hallway who will help you," Carissa explained.

Mrs. O'Brien took her hand, and Cari helped lift her out of the sofa chair. With a "thank you," the older woman left the room. The sidhe followed behind her.

"How did you do that?" Cari asked before he could leave.

"Sidhe magic," he replied unhelpfully.

"But what spell, exactly? How did you call on the magic?"

"Spells are tricks, we do not use them. There is a part of yourself that exists without any layers—no emotion, no thought, no persona. It holds the most powerful magic."

"Like instinct?"

The guard tilted his head. "Something like instinct. But humans think of that word as a reaction. Your deepest self takes over when you need it most—that's the part of you that is magic."

"My deepest self?" Carissa wondered.

Her instincts usually meant her elf side. But that magic she knew was tied to her emotions. Was the Tuatha de Danann side her deeper self? Or was the magic of the most ancient race simply linked to the deepest part of herself?

"Know yourself. The magic will follow."

The sidhe guard left the room. Carissa and Chaos continued their search. At the end of the hall, there was a room that at first appeared empty. Carissa would have checked the bathroom first, as she had in all the other rooms, except that she could see a pair of feet on the floor by the bed. There was a Mossie lying on the other side of the room. Carissa sprang past the bed to see figure curled slightly as if he'd been kicked.

It was Cameron. She dropped down beside him and put a hand on his shoulder. He was out cold, the troll dust covering his whole body. Carissa turned him onto his back.

"Okay, instinct," she said to herself. "Know who I am, how hard can that be?"

She tried clearing her mind. First, she kept her eyes closed. Then, she stared at her hands. After a while, she sighed.

"Who am I, Chaos?"

She looked at the nature faerie, feeling a bit lost. Chaos raised her palms to the ceiling and shrugged. She didn't know. Carissa rose to her feet.

"We'd better find a sidhe guard."

"There you are," Perla said.

Carissa saw her enter. A few paces into the room, Carissa saw the restroom door move but was not fast enough to warn Perla. An "ugh" escaped the troll woman's lips and she dropped out of sight on the other side of the bed.

"Perla!" Cari cried out.

She leaped to her aid, positioning herself between the victim and whoever was on the other side of the bathroom door. Perla lay sprawled on the floor. She quickly regained consciousness and cradled her head in pain.

"Are you all right?" Cari briefly turned to look at her injured friend.

On the floor, Perla uttered the two words that finally caused Carissa's instincts to kick in.

"Behind you!"

Carissa turned and thrust her hands out. The troll's green light hit a rose gold shield. Carissa kept her hands up, struggling to maintain her power against the energy flowing from her attacker.

Why was this difficult? Wasn't a Tuatha de Danaan stronger than a troll? Or was she less powerful, less knowledgeable, or just less than her ancestors?

The shield, almost like a solid object, cracked in small lines all across it. Doubt. If Cari's powers stemmed from the deepest part of herself, she realized that it was doubt in herself that could weaken her. She had to be confident in her abilities. She had to trust herself.

She tensed her fingers, willing herself to be stronger, not physically, but mentally. She let herself believe that she had already won. It was just a matter of acting out what was inevitably going to happen.

The troll's power weakened. The green light dimmed in intensity. Eventually, the green dissolved. Carissa could see right through her shield.

The face looking at her from the other side was Cameron's. Through the rosy shield, Cam's eyes met hers. He winced and clutched his side in pain. Her protection wavered, like a bubble about to burst.

"It's not him," Perla reminded her.

The troll in Cameron's form reached out to her. With Cameron lying just a few feet away, the troll was not fooling Carissa for even a second. He had to think that, though, so that he would believe he had the advantage when she lowered her shield. She couldn't use the protective field and attack him at the same time.

She let go of the rose gold barrier and hit him square in the chest. She didn't use all of her force. She wasn't sure how much power she had and would not risk killing him. Even an unseelie troll's death would carry weight on her conscience she didn't want to have to bear.

It didn't seem like enough, though. He remained on his feet. His hand was on his heart, and he was breathing heavily, but he still eyed Carissa from his standing position. It was unclear whether he would attack, but Carissa would be ready if he did. Her rose gold light had not left her.

She had no need for it at that moment. Chaos, with an adorable karate kick, hit him full force in the jaw. The troll crashed into the wall and fell to the ground. The sound caught the attention of two sidhe, who entered the room to drag the troll away.

"Well done," Carissa told Chaos.

"That sprite is strong for her size," Perla commented.

"You have no idea," Carissa said.

Chaos took the compliments with a bow. As much as the sprite might have liked to relish the praise, Carissa's attention switched immediately to Cameron. The Tuatha de Danann magic was vibrant when she knelt beside Cam. She placed a hand over his heart and closed her eyes.

She didn't think. She didn't allow her emotions to overwhelm her. She just let herself be there with him, the deepest part of herself flowing from her heart to his. Within moments, there was the pure feeling of two heartbeats completely in sync with one another.

Cam's body warmed. Carissa opened her eyes and watched the troll dust evaporate. Blood flowed back into Cameron's face. With a sharp gasp, he awakened.

"The mayor's a troll!" he shouted.

Chaos made that chiming sound she did when she was chuckling, and Perla chortled alongside her. Cari bit her lip and then smiled.

"We know," Carissa said.

"Cari?" Cam looked around, taking in his surroundings. "Where...what...how did I....?"

He struggled to speak. Finally, he stopped and looked into Carissa's eyes. Smiling, he voiced the perfect question.

"Did you save me?"

Chaos flew between them, nodding her head with a grin. She sprinted around Carissa's head, pushing her face closer to Cam.

Carissa laughed, inches away from his lips.

"I did," she said. The sprite flew around the other side, bringing Cam closer to her.

"My hero," Cameron said.

Carissa and Cam found the rest of the way to a kiss without any more help from Chaos.

# Chapter 21

## Valentines

Valentine's Day deserved a redo. Cameron suggested rebooking at the fanciest restaurant in town, but the Rose Garden was not a place she wanted to visit again anytime soon. Besides that, she wasn't much for lavish, over-the-top dinners. If she had a choice of any place in the world, she would choose to eat at the Second Street Pub, surrounded by all of her friends.

Cam had smiled when she said that. He arranged for everyone to meet the day after their harrowing ordeal. Seated in a booth together by a large window in the front, Carissa and Cam greeted their friends as they entered.

The place filled before long with lively chatter and stories shared between tables. The Harbridges arrived early. Cari and Cam found them sitting at a table with Barnaby, Holly, and even Mrs. Alcott and her brownie boarder, Gilly. Timmy had brought a couple of friends along from school for the meal.

Chaos, Hiya, and Cynth saw the coloring papers stacked in front of Timmy and his friends. They invited themselves to color since the kids weren't. Though the two boys and one girl might've been too old for the crayons, they were thrilled that the sprites, who were far older than them in terms of maturity, were coloring. They giggled at Hiya and Cynth arguing over the red crayon. Chaos was more interested in the same thing Carissa had noticed.

The children were still wearing the charms around their necks. The two boys wore stars, the girl a heart. Carissa felt she had to say something.

"You know, you don't have to wear those anymore. The danger's gone."

Timmy looked at his friends and back at Cari. "I gave them away as friendship necklaces. Does it matter that they're magic?"

Carissa knelt so she was eye level with Timmy and smiled.

"That makes them even more magical," she said.

"How can we thank you, Carissa?" Mrs. Harbridge asked.

"Actually, there is something you can do."

Cari's eyes drifted to a man and woman talking with each other outside the pub windows. Her reluctant guests seemed to be enjoying each other's company and avoiding coming inside. Carissa put a finger up for Mrs. Harbridge to hold that thought. She caught the woman's eye and waved her inside.

The pair walked in, glancing nervously around. A few eyes turned to the woman as her color began shifting to green. Carissa made her way behind the tylwyth teg and put her hands on her arms.

"It's okay, don't be nervous," Carissa's soft voice aimed for soothing as she pushed her along.

"Oh, am I doing it again?" the woman asked.

"You're going goblin, my love," her date said.

Once at the Harbridge's table, Carissa stopped and cleared her throat.

"This is Tabitha, and this is Otto Crimbal. They don't go out much. I wonder if you could introduce them to a few people tonight?" she asked.

Patsy and Timothy Harbridge Sr. looked at each other. Tabitha's tylwyth teg nature was hard for her to hide. She kept changing from human shades of skin to full-on green. It wasn't so much off-putting to Mossies as it would be to any tourists who might happen to be in the restaurant. Cari bit her lip, hoping this was not a bad idea. The Harbridges weren't snobs, not entirely, but they did tend to think about things like that.

Timmy broke the ice. He reached over and took the tylwyth teg's hand. "Tabitha's really nice. She helped look after me when you were gone," he said.

Tabitha's shade deepened to a warm tan. She smiled, and Crimbal took her other hand.

"Well, of course," Mr. Harbridge set down his napkin and motioned for the kids to scoot over. "You're more than welcome to join us."

Tabitha squealed in delight, pulling Cari into a hug before sitting. Timmy offered her the last roll in the bread basket. She immediately took the entire bin and began filling it with the other appetizers on the table.

Carissa shook her head. Somehow, she doubted Tabitha would ever blend in. Cari rather liked her that way.

More and more of their friends arrived. Nan happily surprised her by bringing Declan and Perla Greer. From all the way across the room, Perla held up her glass the moment she caught Cari's eye. Carissa held up her own and nodded her acknowledgment. She was glad to have earned a new friend.

Carissa's heart flowed up to her lips, curving them into a smile. She was filled to the brim with happiness before they'd even started their meal. She looked up at Cam. His face held a smile, but his eyes lacked their usual radiance.

"What's wrong?" Carissa asked.

Cameron hesitated. Then he slid his plate aside. "When I invited Varick today, he said that you followed a troll through the forest alone. I've been trying not to think about it. I know you're part fae and you're strong and daring, and I shouldn't worry about you, but I do. You could've been killed. Why did you put yourself in danger like that?"

"Because it was you," Carissa said. "That's not a choice, is it? To leave the hotel and let the man I love die? I couldn't let that happen."

He paused. A transformation came over him. He wasn't even smiling, not fully, but there was a tenderness in his eyes. Quietly, he said, "You love me?"

She shifted her eyes, suddenly self-conscious. Why did he have to turn all serious like that? And the depth in his cognac eyes, it was overwhelming.

"Of course I do," she said. "You know I do."

He linked a hand gingerly with her fingers.

"You've never said it before."

She laughed as if brushing away the thought, but her hand remained. "I'm sure I have."

"I would remember," he said.

A quick glance in his direction showed that the intensity in his stare had not waned. She didn't look away this time.

"Cam," she said. She breathed in and gathered her resolve to repeat the words—and more. "I do love you, but I worry. Look at Jane and Varick. He's going to live forever. She won't. Not unless she takes the elixir of immortality, which he wasn't supposed to give her in the first place. And even if the sidhe agree to it—"

"You're worried you'll outlive me?"

"Yes," she said honestly. "I'm not immortal, but I will live to at least two hundred years." She didn't add the words if the unseelie don't get me out of the way.

"So? Give me the elixir then, a life-enhancing one, an immortality one. Whatever you want. I'll take it," he said.

"Just like that?"

"Why not? Two years, two hundred, or an eternity: I'm with you for however long of a life we have together." He put a hand to his neck, characteristically Cameron. "Obviously, I'll try to be conscious for most of it."

She chuckled. He leaned forward and kissed her. His eyes sparkled as they pulled away. Then, he cleared his throat.

"Cari, since I was unconscious for our last date, I had something planned to give to you." He pulled out a box, a red-velvet one, the perfect size to hold a ring.

"Cam," Carissa said, "I don't think I'm ready for—"

He held up a hand. Then, he laid the box flat on the table. "Just open it," he said.

She glanced between him and the box, then, slowly, she picked it up and held it in her hand, opening the lid.

Inside was a silver ring shaped into a crown set atop two hands holding a heart.

"A Claddagh ring?" she looked up at him with a raised brow.

"Friendship, love, and loyalty," he smiled. The three symbolic images, a heart for love, hands for friendship, and crown for loyalty, glistened under the pub's lighting.

"It's beautiful."

She admired the sight of him taking in her reaction. His grin didn't look the same as when they were kids or even the way he'd looked to her just months ago. When she saw him now, he looked a lot less like the schoolmate she'd grown up with and much more like the man she was going to marry. She remembered what Maren had told her.

"You were going to ask me something?"

Cam cleared his throat. "Um, yes, I was."

Carissa enjoyed the way his eyes shifted nervously around the table. She relished the way he took both of her hands into his own. And when he stared into her eyes, all her doubts melted away. She was sure her answer was going to be a "yes."

"Cari, how would you feel about...."

The irritating pause made it feel like her heart was going to leap out of her chest. She had to concentrate just to keep her elf-light from causing sparks between their fingers. She held her breath.

"...Me running for mayor?"

Carissa's mouth fell open. She blinked. Her ears twitched to make sure she had heard that right.

"How would I feel about you running for mayor?" she repeated.

Cameron let go of her hand and turned his glass in one hand. He smoothed out the tablecloth anxiously with the other.

"Yes. See, I have a lot of ideas, and I was starting to disagree with Mayor Belkin, back when, you know, we didn't realize he was a troll. Of course, now we don't actually have a mayor, so the council will have to choose someone before the term is officially over in May."

"Who's filling in until then?"

Cam grinned.

"You are?" Carissa realized.

His smile grew. He leaned forward. "So, what do you think?"

Mossies had decided years ago to hold direct elections for their mayors rather than allowing the city council to choose one. This made May an exciting time for voting citizens. It might make Carissa's life a lot more complicated. She smiled anyway.

"I think you should follow your dream," she told him.

Cam placed a palm over the Claddagh ring on Cari's hand. "It's only a dream if you're in it with me."

"Hey, listen to this," Maren walked to the table with a pint in one hand and her phone in the other. She nearly dropped the frothy drink on seeing the ring on Cari's finger.

"Ooh, he gave it to you! Isn't it neat?" she asked, seating herself next to Cari without invitation. She grabbed Carissa's hand and admired the ornament. Cam and Carissa looked at each other after a minute.

"You were saying?" Carissa reminded her why she'd come over to them.

"Oh, right." Maren dropped the hand and picked up her phone from the table. "Tilly just posted this on her blog:

"*Mossies and Madness: Posted February 17*

'*The recent string of events in Moss Hill nearly resulted in stringing up an innocent faerie woman from the Village of Vale. I never thought I'd see the day when Mossies would storm a home like a medieval mob. Before the madness was over, we were pointing fingers at each other without looking at the people on the other end of the accusations we flung.*

'*Carissa Shae of the Seelie Tree Apothecary cured us of the near-fatal disease of discord the changelings inflicted upon us. She saw through the masks we all should have noticed because we know each other. We didn't have to question who the changelings were—it was evident in the actions they performed.*

*'They called for separation from our fae neighbors. They made us fear each other. They asked us for a supply of all the hatred we were willing to give. They changed who we are. And they did this by using the greatest weapon in evil's arsenal: fear. The brutal truth is that the fear will rise. The sidhe guard has confirmed that the increase in unseelie presence on the island is likely to continue. So, what do we do?*

*'We don't let go of each other. We are an island built on friendship and the premise that humans and fae of all kinds can live here together in peace. So, instead of spreading fear and hate, we will spread hope and love. Because that's what we do in Moss Hill. That is what makes us Mossies.'"*

"Powerful," Cam said. "I hope people take it to heart."

"I certainly will," Maren replied. She put her arm out to catch Holly as the fae woman walked back to the Harbridge's with Barnaby. "I'm sorry I was less than welcoming to you at the Seelie Tree. I'm glad we had you with us this last week."

She opened her arms wide. Holly blushed and gave her a hug as she balanced her refreshment in her hand. Barnaby grinned through his own glass.

"Oh, never you worry, dear. It's my pleasure to help," Holly said.

"She's a real treasure, this one. I'm glad we found each other again," Barnaby added.

Holly deepened in shade. She let Barnaby kiss her hand. The two of them squeezed into the booth next to Cameron. The pub's doors opened, drawing attention from all five of them.

"Well, I guess Jane and Varick are back together," Maren noted.

The door opened again to reveal Alden. He took down the hood of his jacket. He was in human form but still seemed uncomfortable out in public. There was no going back after he'd revealed himself at the hotel. People knew he was ankou now.

Carissa wondered how his parents were taking his undead presence back in their lives. They'd be happy, Carissa hoped. He might be breaking MacLir's rules, but now that she was beginning to realize her Tuatha de Danann magic, maybe there was something she could do about that. For now, Alden seemed happy—uncomfortable maybe, but happy. He walked between Jane and Varick as they made their way to a table near the rest of their friends.

There were small signs of love between Varick and Jane—a smile, a passing look. But there was not the overwhelming passion of a romance. They were strengthening another side to their relationship first: friendship.

Carissa said, "Maybe Jane and Varick will be together one day, but not yet. People need to know themselves before they can love somebody else."

"Love takes time." Maren sighed. "I guess that's my problem. Falling too fast."

"So, you're taking it slower with Reg?"

"I'm in 'like' with him. He's a decent guy. We'll see how things go when he gets back to Moss Hill. His last letter said he'd be back in April, which reminds me...." Maren pulled a letter out of her purse. "This came for you at the Seelie Tree."

Carissa raised an eyebrow as she opened the envelope. The signature caught her eye first.

"It's from Raven Corvus."

"The one who sent you Chaos?"

Carissa nodded.

"Read it out loud," Cameron said.

Carissa read, *"Well done, my dears. I may have enlisted you, Carissa, but this letter applies as much to the ankou, the druidess, the ambassador, the human, and the faeries who've helped you. You've managed this far to succeed against several types of unseelie fae—from bansidhes to hobgoblins. Now, you've gone against troll changelings and won. This is no small accomplishment. But, the worst is yet to come. I am coming—and I'm sorry. Where I go, trouble follows. Be prepared for unseelie like you've never seen before. Be prepared for me."*

"Is she making a threat?" Cam asked.

"She's giving a warning," Holly replied.

"A warning of what?" Barnaby asked with a quiver in his voice.

"Whatever it is, we'll be ready," Carissa assured.

Holly raised her glass in the air. "Of course we will, we have a Tuatha de Danann."

"Here, here," Barnaby seconded the emotion and raised his own glass.

"No, let's not drink to just one person." Carissa raised her glass. "To friendship."

"To friendship," the others all chimed in.

Cam raised his glass a second time. "And to love."

Carissa and Cam clinked their glasses together. Barnaby clacked his pint into the two of theirs and said happily, "To friendship and love."

Holly rolled her eyes at his inability to grasp that he'd interrupted a private moment. Carissa smiled at her. Then, her eyes caught Cam's as he laughed and put his arm around the leprechaun.

The rest of the pub seemed to hear their toast. One by one, the patrons of the Second Street Pub raised their glasses. The call of "to friendship and love" resounded among the crowd like a call to arms. Looking over the tables at her friends and neighbors, Carissa wasn't worried about Ms. Corvus's latest note. They could get through anything together.

That is what made them Mossies.

# Want more great content?

Hi, I'm Astoria Wright, the author of The Faerie Apothecary Cozy Mysteries. I hope you've enjoyed Charms and Changelings.

## Check out the rest of
## The Faerie Apothecary Mysteries:

*Chaos in the Countryside* – A Novella Prequel
Book 1: *Herbs and Homicide*
Book 2: *Remedy and Ruins*
Book 3: *Elixirs and Elves*
Book 4: *Charms and Changelings*
Book 5: *Potions and Panic*
Book 6: *Talismans and Turmoil*
Book 7: *Tonics and Turning Points*

To keep up to date about this series and others by the author, check out the website:

## www.astoriawright.com

Sign up for the mailing list for updates and freebies available only to members!

## A Note from Chaos:

Do you like this book?
I hope you do.
Please do me a favor
and leave a review!
(on Amazon)

## Thanks for reading!